Nothing Like Beirut

The Publishers gratefully acknowledge the support of

The Arts Council / An Chomhairle Ealaíon

and The Arts Council of Northern Ireland.

☞

Nothing Like Beirut

Briege Duffaud

POOLBEG

Published in 1994 by
Poolbeg,
A division of Poolbeg Enterprises Ltd,
Knocksedan House,
123 Baldoyle Industrial Estate,
Dublin 13, Ireland

© Briege Duffaud 1994

The moral right of the author has been asserted.

A catalogue record for this book is available from the British Library.

ISBN 1 85371 361 9

All rights reserved. No part of this publication may be reproduced or transmitted in any form or by any means, electronic or mechanical, including photography, recording, or any information storage or retrieval system, without permission in writing from the publisher. The book is sold subject to the condition that it shall not, by way of trade or otherwise, be lent, resold or otherwise circulated without the publisher's prior consent in any form of binding or cover other than that in which it is published and without a similar condition, including this condition, being imposed on the subsequent purchaser.

Cover painting *Kingdom of Heaven on Earth* by Micky Donnelly
Cover design by Poolbeg Group Services Ltd/Bite Design
Set by Poolbeg Group Services Ltd in Garamond 10/13
Printed by The Guernsey Press Company Ltd,
Vale, Guernsey, Channel Islands.

For my Mother

Some of these stories have appeared in
NEW IRISH WRITING, IMAGE, SHE, and
THE GUARDIAN

CONTENTS

Nothing Like Beirut	1
Innocent Bystanders	16
Things Fall Apart	39
On the Stairs	55
Furniture	67
Pièces d'Identité	79
Escape	90
A Novel about the Famine	103
Beggars Upon Horseback	120
An Exorcism	132
Swan Song	141
Mixed Marriage	151
The Prize	166

Nothing Like Beirut

THEY WERE OUT THERE IN THE RAIN, THE FOUR OF THEM, NOT marching or anything, just slogging along miserably in the grey Easter drizzle. We were in the lighted dining-room, nice and warm round the table in front of the picture window, drinking Liebfraumilch, looking out at them without much curiosity or friendliness or anything else.

It had given me a bit of a turn all the same, seeing them appear round the corner by the two big sycamore trees and march through the scented rosebush of my childhood. Four British soldiers marching like an insult through the rosebush of my safe and scented childhood, through the mammy-daddy-grannyness of a small pampered world where every smile of mine was an exhibition, every cry brought a regiment running to rescue me.

It was only then that I noticed the rosebush was gone. I'd forgotten all about it for years, until memory showed me the soldiers marching through it. The sycamores were gone too, cut down long ago when their roots were seen to be invading the foundations of the new bungalow. And the soldiers were not even marching: I sat with a piece of garlic bread halfway to my mouth and watched them trail raggedly down the meadow in the nagging rain.

"What are they looking for?" I asked resentfully. "What do they think they're going to find, *here* of all places?"

"Oh trust our Kathleen to get all sentimental about her wee green fields!" Teresa jeered, "And did no-one ever *tell* you about Bandit Country, dear?"

"It's just a routine patrol," Imelda was reassuring me. "They come this way regularly. It's a short cut back to the barracks."

An Easter Sunday patrol trailing through Spring drizzle while we sat in the lighted dining-room eating roast lamb and broccoli and garlic bread. Drinking common-market Liebfraumilch: the parochial innocence of our rural childhood being, after all, as far back in the past as the vanished rosebush.

They'd like you to think it was Beirut or some place.

That's what I always did think at first, returning after a long absence, knowing it only from media clichés. On the afternoon shuttle they served cream teas, the hostess smiled and smiled like anywhere and, waiting for Imelda and John to pick me up at the airport, I could buy Jeffrey Archer like anywhere. Better than anywhere: I could buy Seamus Heaney too. But for an hour or so my manipulated brain still always expected Beirut or Baghdad or San Salvador, expected it till I was driven sixty peaceful miles to this safe townland of forsythia in gardens and tractors busy in tiny hedged fields, and the bogs and the lake and the hills of always. Without the sheltering trees now, without the roses, but nothing like Beirut all the same I thought, with some resentment, watching armed soldiers patrol our innocent empty meadow.

Every few years we spend a holiday together in the house where my sister Imelda now lives quietly with her quiet schoolteacher husband. Two old spinsters and an old bachelor, we joke, back looking for the warmth of the cradle. Not that Bill is a bachelor. He has an English wife who refuses to set foot, he explained once, in a country where war is being waged against her. She evidently believes the media clichés too. Or maybe it's just that she despises us. Bill married above him, lives in Esher in a Tudor-style house, has a daughter at boarding-school near Brighton. Nor could you call Teresa exactly a spinster either. She is active in the trade union movement and in a Dublin feminist group, has a long standing, not-quite-secret affair with a married Labour politician.

I'm the only old maid, if one must use such a term, living alone in a Kilburn bedsit, teaching Survival English to refugees from various Third World upheavals. (A suitable job for a survivor, I once remarked flippantly and then, appalled, began for the first time to ponder the gory drama of *their* survival compared with the almost cosy banality of my own.)

Our parents died fifteen years ago, in a car crash, on holiday. Their first car, their first holiday. When it happened I was in a drugs clinic, on the edge of recovery. The people in charge, seeing my shock, listening to my hopeless bereft sobbing, feared I might regress. I didn't. To everyone's surprise I left the clinic shortly afterwards feeling strong and free, went to college to train as a teacher and, eventually, found this job with the refugee aid centre.

After the tragedy our younger brothers and sisters scattered, married, lost touch. We'd never been a united family; looking back on it now, we seem to have spent most of our childhood snapping and jostling for crumbs of an overworked mother's attention.

Perhaps all large families are like that? If we four older ones keep in contact it may be because we began our lives in an era less crowded with sibling rivalries. I, the eldest, am the only one who can recall a time of real privilege, of being a pampered only child in a pretty thatched cottage surrounded by sycamore trees and roses. It can only have lasted three or four years but it's those few years I remember when I think of my childhood. At intervals throughout my life when I've run back home for comfort it's those quiet years I've been running towards, and never quite reaching. It was regret for those sheltered years that invaded me as I watched the soldiers invading our meadows on Easter Sunday ...

My grandmother's lap was as broad as a bed, as broad as the world, as broad as the pram where they put me to sleep on a summer day beside the scented rosebush. The roses waved down at me; I smiled back in love, mistaking them for something unchangingly eternal, part of the mammy-daddy-granniness of my world. Slowly in the fierce summer I saw them turn brown and die and disappear. In the July heat they placed my pram under the shade of the two big sycamores and hairy brown caterpillars fell on me, fell on the pram, advanced across the sheet making for me, making for my face, my eyes, open mouth. I roared and roared in terror, keep them away, don't let them get me! Caesar the collie jumped up barking, bewildered, his front paws flat on my chest. He was a friend, he was part of the mammy-daddy-granny, he would turn away the brown advancing crawling things. But he didn't. He couldn't. He kept on barking in time to my roars. The regiment came running: two from the house, Daddy up from the meadow with a scythe in his hand, Ned Maginn and big Paddy Mickle were over the ditch like athletes, the dog, oh the bleddy old dog, he has the life scared out of the child, get on you blaggard get out of it! Ah poor wee Kathleen what's on you at all at all? It's only Caesar, sure he wouldn't touch you, it's only playing he was.

And I was lifted and kissed (the poor wee face of her drowned wet with the crying, she must have wakened out of some oul' dream and seen the dog), crushed against the soft flowery overall, passed on to the black satiny dress, jogged on the daddy's shoulders, caterpillars crawling on my white summer frock: look Kathleen, look at all the funny wee animals, look at all the God's horses, Kathleen, feel their nice furry coats! And I couldn't stop roaring, a caterpillar on my mother's finger, rearing itself up on my mother's finger, straight under my eyes: I couldn't stop roaring. So they gave me gripewater in case my wee stomach was upset: that's what it must have been, some pain or another! I sobbed without hope from the inside depth of myself, hiding my face in my granny's black shoulder while they tried to distract and pacify me with the plague of hairy God's horses that fell from the sycamore trees.

When the sobs turned to exhausted sleep they took me in and put me in the cradle and I woke hours later to the soft yellow lamp hanging on a nail, to the three of them sitting round the fire talking quietly so as not to disturb me, to the shadows moving on the dresser, a plate coming to life out of nothing as the flames jumped, then another and another, then a mug and a shiny teapot, a clasp in my mother's hair, and the brown crawling things might never have happened, they'd changed nothing. And I stretched and called and they ran with smiles and warm milk and spoonfuls of gruel; that's what they'd been waiting for. That's all they existed for, kind and ignorant, to wait for my call, to minister to me, to spring gratefully into life when my flame touched them. Somewhere, walled up in the cellars of my mind, God's horses galloped towards me across a white sheet and no one in my world knew the importance of stopping them ...

"Something wrong with that garlic bread?" Teresa joked aggressively. "If you saw yourself sitting there like an eejit, staring at it!"

"Oh sorry!" I slid confusedly back over nearly forty years, "Sorry. I was just thinking about those guys out there. Isn't it strange, I mean how we could never think of asking them in to shelter till the rain stops. And when we were kids wouldn't it have been unthinkable *not* to ask them?"

"God above! Easy to see some of us live safe in London. Want to get poor Imelda and John kneecapped do you? Ach would you look at them! Would you look at the cut of our brave boys, hopping like four wee frogs along the fence. Jolly good old chepp!" she jeered in a Wodehouse accent, "*Oooh* well done, Bertie old boy!"

The soldiers were picking careful steps out of the squelchy ground alongside the overgrown turf bog, making stepping-stones out of a row of half-sunk paling posts, a relic of my parents' time, when cattle grazed the meadow. They looked depressed, looked incredibly lonely, each member of the little group enclosed in the solitude of his down-pointed weapon, of his boots squelching and sucking at the alien marshland, his unquiet awareness of our eyes watching him from the bungalow windows. Of his knowledge that if death came blasting out of those windows it would come to no occupying army: it would come to him alone, unshared, blast him cold and alone out of his island of cold wet aloneness.

But the bungalow windows were neutral. We sat in the warm lighted dining-room and watched these four young men with blackened faces moving through the grey drizzle. They might have been on a television screen, the turf bog some dreary alien landscape, for all the connection there was between them and us. Yet, in my childhood, when turf was dug there every summer, my mother used to talk from the window to the shirt-sleeved straining diggers, to a passing neighbour, to a child wandering too near the water. The friendly shouted phrases, cutting into meditation or fatigue or discouragement, were a cheerful denial of human solitude.

Now we poured wine, passed sauce boat and vegetable dish while our eyes, empty of friendliness or hostility, watched the four men take an old turf-cutters' path and move tensely in the rain between the alder bushes and the tall marsh plants.

I wondered if those old places that I loved were to them hostile enemy territory, if they really expected or feared to come upon some deadly peril lurking among the tufted beds of rushes where I played as a child? I wondered too if they noted in passing the promise of new life just becoming visible in a landscape that was emerging from a long fierce winter – the nesting waterfowl, the soft resurrected green of the pussy-willows. Or if their eyes had by now evolved into nothing more than the eyes of small wild creatures, hunters or hunted, alert only to prey or to concealed danger? If I'd been alone I would have smiled, or wept, recalling lost summer days exploring those paths, watching armed men skirt the broad fringed lake and make for the rising meadows beyond the bog.

"How are the ducks getting on?" I asked.

Last time I was home the conservation people were creating a bird sanctuary, planting the lake with some species of rare duck; an effort to raise local morale, they said, and give the region another identity than the cruel dismissive one forced on it by newspaper headlines.

"Did they settle in all right? I suppose they'd be nesting by now?"

"Those ducks weren't given much chance to settle in." John spoke roughly. "Vandals got hold of those ducks. It was disgusting, the whole place was disgusted. They were found scattered along the far end of the lake one morning. In bits. Wings cut off. Eyes gouged out. Christ it was ... "

"Some pervert," Imelda said. "Nobody was ever got for it."

"Or maybe someone high on drugs?" Teresa asked.

"No, there's not too much of that round here, the boys keep a sharp eye out for dealers. Say what you like about the Provos, Kath, but you of all people must agree that ... "

"But *who*? And why? They were beautiful, why on earth would anyone?"

More shaken than I'd ever been by any of the screaming headlines I looked out over the lake again, seeing it in darkness, picturing some lonely rejected failure of a man, some mute inglorious Rambo, crouched in his solitude away over there by the water's edge, an open knife in one hand, a trembling wet body gripped at his mercy in the other, ejaculating his shame and his despair among the new green willows. Is that what it would have been like? Or had it been just some noisy jostling group of youngsters out for an evening, a bit drunk maybe, gang-banging away the frustrations of some empty limited life that had never been warmed by roses or sheltering trees or affection? Would they have been united afterwards in a wink of complicity, gloating over a few pints in one of the pubs? Why not? Why assume some lonely hidden shame? Or imagine that outrage is inevitably denied public acceptance? Well of course it's not, I thought, isn't outrage allowed to strut and boast proudly in the open, here and everywhere else?

"For all we know," John said dourly, "For all we know it could even be a crowd of them lads out there. It's not because a man's in uniform ... The whole country's crawling with trash these days, I tell you. Dirty trash!" Glasses shocked slightly against plates as his fist came down firmly on the white tablecloth, surprising us. "Sorry," he muttered.

"Oh let's not get carried away about a few dead ducks," Teresa said coolly. "Other places they do it to children, you know. To women. All those poor kids in England, those women raped and mutilated." My refugees too, with stories

Nothing Like Beirut

of unimaginable horror walled up behind their smiles ...

"You know those slogans," I said, "that we saw coming through Belfast, Imelda? VENCEREMOS! and PROVISIONAL IRA AGAINST APARTHEID! Weren't they monstrous? Do you not think they were monstrous?"

"And what was so monstrous about them?" Teresa turned on me in sharp disapproval.

"Well, I mean at first I thought the IRA was protesting about South Africa, I really did, and I was thinking well, gosh that's something, at least they're not *always* peering into their own bellybuttons, and then when John said what they really meant was the apartheid that's supposed to be forced on us by the Prods ... Well I mean it's unreal isn't it, it's a *joke*, it's just paranoid?"

"Monstrous. Paranoid. What big words you've got, Kathleen! So what's all that got to do with dead ducks for God's sake?"

I might have known, but I tried anyway to explain how the slogans shocked me because they'd been stolen from people whose everyday lives were passed in the shadow of death squad and secret police and extermination camp, of famine and massacre and genocide.

"What I mean is," I said into their cold attentive silence, "Well like I mean that hero who painted his wee VENCEREMOS on the Falls Road Belfast knew damn well he didn't risk being tortured to death for painting it, now didn't he? Oh forget it," I trailed off weakly, knowing that I would not find words to make them see a possible connection between the empty boastful slogans and the pathetic futility of the dead birds. I never do find the right words when I'm at home among them, I never have done. Time and again I've seen perfectly sane ideas wither into sentimental nothings confronted with Teresa's assertive militancy and the lopsided neutrality of the others. It was stupid to mention the slogans, they weren't all that significant anyhow, except to a squeamish outsider. Just clever graffiti. And the birds, as Imelda said, had been killed by some anonymous pervert. There *was* no real connection.

I helped my sisters clear the table and carry in the pavlova and dessert plates from the kitchen. The four soldiers moved through the rain past the lake where the birds were murdered, reached the dry land on Bogan's meadow, and began to climb slowly up out of the valley.

"Do you remember gathering blackberries in Bogan's fields?" I asked, forcing the lines of my face to relax and soften, deliberately walling the outrage away behind a barricade of memories, as I recalled wet August grass slapping bare legs, the treachery of a trailing bramble that got you round the ankle, the heroic sting of blood, bony arms scarred and purpled, the triumph of a brimming full bucket.

"Oh here we go again," Teresa jeered. "She's off! She's off! Birth of a Naturalist yet!"

Imelda smiled at me: "Yeah I suppose it was all right at the time but let's face it Kath, what about going back to the Convent every September with our hands and wrists all scratched, getting it rubbed in that the other kids didn't earn their winter uniforms picking fruit round the hedges? God I really hated those berries from about the age of twelve on!"

"*I* didn't hate the *berries*," Teresa announced, "I hated the other kids, the spoiled gets of shopkeepers' daughters who sneered at us. All those wee local Maggie Thatchers who never did make it. Actually I was quite proud of earning money that way. I made damn sure *I* sneered back at *them*!"

"Oh trust you," Bill said sourly. "Our Teresa the big revolutionary, making enemies wherever she goes."

I recalled that Bill, when he got his first promotion in

the bank, took golfing lessons and joined the local country club. We hide our scars the best way we can, I thought, and looked back out of the window at the gentle landscape of my childhood, and at armed soldiers trudging uphill through it now in the relentless rain.

I remembered the Easter I came home with scars to hide. It had not been raining then. April was unusually warm that year, 1968 it was, but I had to wear a long-sleeved jersey all through the holiday to hide the needle-tracks on my bony arms. I was eighteen and, recognising in a moment of lucidity the danger of the monsters that were making for me, I'd come panicking home to the sanctuary of roses and sheltering trees.

"You don't look well at all," my mother said. "Don't go back to London, child, stay here for a bit and I'll look after you. If you're in jeopardy for God's sake tell me and I'll look after you."

An offer to remember for life: if you're in jeopardy I'll look after you. A mother's uncomprehending promise of everlasting protection. She thought I was pregnant and was loyally prepared to brave local opinion and see me through it, not realising that what I needed was far more, and at the same time far less, than that. But I thought about her offer all day. The bungalow had not yet been built; the old cottage with its deep thatch, with its sycamore trees and roses, seemed the solidest of havens, my parents the mightiest of protectors.

Then in the night I woke sobbing from a confused frightened dream and heard mice running along the rafters: help me please help me someone they put me in a room with rats, my half-asleep mind transforming my mother and father into the monsters they might well have been, anyone might well be. For how can you know, I lay thinking, how can you possibly trust yourself into anyone's power? Which had surprised me even as I thought it, recalling how my happiest safest time had been when I was small and helpless and completely in their power. I lay awake until dawn, trembling and anxious, but when early light transfigured the room into home I realised that it had only been mice and that they had always been there, harmless and familiar, a part of my childhood.

Later that day, as we sat on chairs under the sycamore trees in the warmth of that lovely unusual Easter, I smiled with gratitude, examining the idea of living there, of moving peacefully through my adult life in those small rooms that looked out on small fields and turf bog and lake and sycamore trees, a protected child again in a small pampered world, my parents kind and ignorant ministering to my needs. But knowing that it was too late to be a child because I was eighteen years old and because they were too kind, and too ignorant, to suspect what monsters were making for me, what scars were hidden under the smiles and the long-sleeved jersey.

The soldiers were four shapeless bumps nearing the horizon now. They would cross up Dog Moloney's big field, climb over the stone wall, and find themselves in a narrow primrosed lane that dipped down to the main road.

"The way we used to go to Mass, remember, when we were small, picking primroses and pegging stones at Moloney's alsatians. Will you ever forget the roars of those alsatians! And when you look back on it, what did he need them for? What had he that needed guarding any more than the rest of us?"

"He was just an old sadist that's all, getting his kicks out of scaring the neighbours. He wasn't right in the head, sure he half-starved those dogs and then threatened his wife with them when he was drunk. Wasn't that why they had to be put down in the end, they near tore an arm off her. Remember how the police were out and everything. She was in the hospital for ages."

"I never knew that," I said. "Nobody ever told me that."

Bill laughed: "Well then, you must have been the only one in the country *didn't* know it!"

Teresa turned on me sarcastically: "Oh, Kath wouldn't have *wanted* to know it. Our Kath probably had herself convinced that old Moloney was a nice beardy leprechaun and the dogs were just wee woolly toys, isn't that it, Kathleen?"

I was about to make a joking comeback when I noticed her eyes and they weren't joking at all, they were quite cold and contemptuous. For the first time, I recognised that my sister's constant jeers had nothing to do with children harmlessly snapping and teasing at each other: they were real, and she disliked me with a real, adult, dislike.

I wondered with a sudden little chill, if there had ever been any genuine liking among the four of us, or if we were united only by the scars of our shared childhood. I became uneasily aware too that of *course* I'd known about Dog Moloney's wife. People had talked about nothing else for weeks. I'd been eleven or twelve at the time and, Sunday after Sunday, we'd gone to Mass in fascinated horror, Teresa searching avidly for lingering bloodstains behind the wall. Then, I suppose, I'd made myself forget.

"Dogs or no dogs," I said defensively, "I always enjoyed walking to Mass and so did you. Do you ever go that way now, Imelda?"

"Oh sure nobody walks to Mass these days," she told me. "Nobody uses that old lane now except the army."

"They're welcome to it," Bill said fiercely. "Do you remember the muck up to our ankles for about ten months of the year, and all the town kids laughing at our dirty boots? I suppose you've managed to forget details like that too, Kathleen?"

I didn't answer. I was trying to imagine the place without its alsatians, with nothing at all now to give it a thrill of horror. Just a disused country loaning, old Moloney dead for years, and his house an ivy-covered ruin.

Strung out in a line, the soldiers crossed over the stone wall and dropped out of sight in the old lane. The meadow, the bog, and the lake belonged to me and my childhood again ...

It was several seconds before my mind would admit what was happening, though I, though all of us, could be conscious of nothing but the noise of the explosion roaring and growling and destroying, surging back over the horizon, filling the valley, fading raggedly into the silent rain, giving way to the desolate mourning scream of sirens from the town.

"Well whatever those guys were looking for they seem to have found," Teresa said with a short laugh.

Imelda glanced quickly sideways at her husband and made the Sign of the Cross. A helicopter lifted itself off from the observation post two miles away, another from the direction of the army barracks. They droned in across the empty lake, the bog, towards the place where clumps of Easter primroses would be blown shattered among the mud.

"That's the most shocking thing of all," I said out loud, and the others looked at me as they always did when I uttered what Teresa called one of my pious clichés. But what I meant was that for nearly an hour I'd been watching those four men walking straight into death through a landscape of lies, through turf-bog and blackberried fields and Mass-going path, through my lost childhood happiness that had never been anything but an illusion. This landscape had always been more violent and less innocent than I'd let myself remember, our house had been poor and overcrowded and ugly with jealousies, the sheltering sycamore trees had never sheltered me.

The others had known it all the time, but what *I'd* let

myself remember was a fairy tale of secure innocence: the beauty of primroses, the way the starving chained-up dogs strained impotently to get us, roaring because *they'd* always be chained and *we'd* always be safe. I'd walled the truth up somewhere: the mud-splashed Sunday stockings, the taunts of a snobbish nun, the very real power of those alsatians chained up just behind Moloney's wall waiting their chance, the winter jersey whose long sleeves never quite hid the scars I earned it with. I'd walled up the roses turning brown and dead, terror falling from the sycamore trees, my parents kind and ignorant, wounding me with their incomprehension.

All the same, watching the helicopters circling in like vultures, I wished and wished above all things that I could be back in a time when there was a rosebush at the corner of a thatched cottage and my mother called jokes to the turf-cutters in the bog, and the horror behind Dog Moloney's wall had not yet broken its chains and got loose. I heard myself stammering something like that to the others, explaining to them that the whole country, the whole world, would give anything to be back in that lovely warm Easter of 1968 when you could still pretend, in the daytime, that it was only mice running along the rafters.

And then, as Teresa shrugged disdainful shoulders and bustled off to make coffee, as Imelda risked another sideglance at her silent husband, I realised I was very probably deluding myself about that as well.

INNOCENT BYSTANDERS

THE FIRE DIED WITH A SOFT SPLASH AND SIGH OF FALLING ASH. HER mother was asleep in the armchair and Helen didn't like to disturb her by going out for more briquettes. It wasn't that cold anyhow. The daughter tried to read and the mother slept on, snoring very slightly. She dropped into sleep easily nowadays; no sooner had the Feeneys left than she settled into the chair and drifted off as if Helen was a thousand miles away. But then the Feeneys would put anyone to sleep, Helen thought, Father Joseph guzzling After Eights and lamenting the desperate changes he saw in Ireland – worse every time he came home, the country entirely given over to the punks and the layabouts. Not to mention the violence, his sister said, it's a holy terror that decent people can't come and go in peace in the town they were reared in, you wouldn't mind them shooting soldiers but the majority of the time it's innocent bystanders that's called on to suffer and what is Ireland coming to?

It had been the same refrain last time Helen was home, over fifteen years earlier, only then it was the miniskirt and the Beatles and how decent people couldn't even go out to Mass without having their eyes assaulted by shameless tramps showing everything they had. Pure vinegar, Miss Feeney, and always was. How in the name of God did Mother put up with her? They seemed to be the best of friends, though it had not always been so. But then mother was shockingly changed, her standards were not the same. There was a slackening, a sort of quiet indifference that made impossible any but the most platitudinous attempt at conversation.

The violent changes round home did not touch Helen at all, she'd come prepared for them: where she lived now the very name of the town she'd grown up in had become a sort of shorthand for terror. What did shock her though was this unexpected picture of her mother in retirement. The slangy clichés holding life at a distance, Dallas on the telly, the synthetic plants and the flowery carpets and the Lourdes water bottled in fluorescent plastic. A Mills and Boon romance jostling the Rosary beads and on the same shelf a few library books and a motheaten copy of *Gone With The Wind*. Helen remembered that being hidden under the mattress long ago when it came in the Yankee parcel, for fear that Miss Feeney might drop in with her holy spying eyes and now here it was out in the open.

Things were changed all right: the very book she was reading, published in Dublin no less, some girl had an abortion in it and no one belonging to her as much as turned a hair! It couldn't have been written the last time she was home, wouldn't have got printed, would have been on the Index or something, Archbishop McQuaid thundering from his pulpit. She was glad of course, oh she wasn't knocking it at all, only it was shutting her out, all this dream world, this JR and *Crossroads* and the splashy fitted carpets and the picture windows. Cur-rist! she thought, the old woman whatever her faults she used to at least talk about real things, she never quit instilling all the virtues into us both at home and at school. Not content with the patriotic trimmings to the Rosary she used to have the lot of us lined up in the classroom reciting "The Rebel" and vowing that we'd do our level best to die for our country like Patrick Pearse who was her great idol. You started off in Infants with Miss Feeney drumming it into you that the only noble destiny was to be a foreign missionary risking your life in a heathen jungle like her own brother, then you got promoted to Mother's class and told what a proud thing it must be to die for Ireland. For your Faith too of course, she was stiff with ideals when I was a kid.

Or am I re-inventing her, Helen wondered, am I busy building myself a folklore? Well she was stuck in the middle of more reality now than she ever bargained for and all she could do was cry over some American shit of a soap-opera and switch off the News with a sighed cliché about what was the world coming to at all at all? And drift off to sleep while her daughter waited in vain for the healing words, the anger and forgiveness, the slap followed by the blessing. Not a word had been spoken so far about Helen's situation, about the years of estrangement, there had been no prodigal's welcome. They went here and there to visit neighbours, exchanged harmless remarks, helped Miss Feeney arrange the house for her reverend brother's holiday. Sometimes Tim came over from Newry for the evening but that was awkward too; they had never got on well. He'd always been a scourge with his jokes and his jeers and now, heading for middle-age, his jokes had razor blades in them. A sour old bachelor. Helen, longing for intimacy, dying to spread out her life for the delight of her family, was forced to sit evening after evening nursing a book in front of a dead fire while her mother dozed. Yet she sent for me, Helen thought, she did send for me.

"You wouldn't know there was a bit of trouble in the country at all." That's what her mother had written a month before, "It's all quiet and peaceful around here, the odd explosion or kidnapping, but sure the half of the time you wouldn't hear a word about it till you saw it on the News." She wrote as she spoke, had always done so. For two decades her words had brought without fail the handful of small rocky fields, the country schoolhouse, turf-bog spread at its feet, Slieve Gullion a distant blue hump, child's mountain-shape hiding no secrets. Brought them as balm or as blame, as ginny tears on a foreign beach, as iconoclastic intruders into a life that occasionally, and at last, promised freedom: this is all you are, this is where you'll end up. Her letters were constantly consoling, insulting, being proud of her clever daughter, ashamed of her, encouraging her, accusing her, twitching her back from the edge of adventure, plucking her out of the centre of some happiness, stopping her hand in the instant of caress. They were a rope, stupid old lifeline/umbilical cord, attaching Helen to her.

Only not to *her*, not to this woman Nellie McCabe, country schoolmarm, whom one knew to be ordinary, warm, funny, ignorant, as wise and as foolish as any woman, as fond of a laugh, of a new dress, a good meal – not to her at all, Helen wouldn't have minded, but to this great and sorrowing institution, The Irish Catholic Mother, and in her mother's case more: Irish Catholic Widowed Mother, with what that implied of martyrdom and sacrifice. Image of course of Our Immaculate Lady who's forever prying into one's mind and heart and going beetroot with shame at what her virgin eyes see there. But image and more so of Mother Erin, that poor unwilling battered wife with her trials and her tribulations, exalted by suffering to a monumental egoism, obsessed to the point of neurosis with her terror of being in the end betrayed by her faithless ungrateful offspring.

The rope had been left lying slack for seven years, ever

since the news of Helen's second marriage. Indeed Helen had believed it cut, and had suffered accordingly. Her mother didn't write at all, not as much as a Christmas card or a line when Caroline was born. When Helen most needed letters, needed blame, praise, encouragement, some proof for godsake that she existed, that she was remembered with warmth by the handful of small fields, well *then* she didn't write. Helen wrote to her explaining, accusing (her intolerance, her narrowmindness and what did you think I was anyway, a bloody nun?), insulting, begging, raging, until finally broken-backed with remorse and loneliness she began to crawl belatedly towards some semblance of maturity.

Then in September, the letter. She wasn't as young as she used to be, a body thinks things over, it was a pity to lose all contact, to keep up old disagreements. She supposed Helen was in the habit of going here and there for her holidays, would she not think of spending a week or two in the Ireland sometime soon and bringing Caroline? There was no danger at all, she need have no worries about bringing the child, sure you'd never know there was a ...

Though Helen knew otherwise – knew that all that Spring and Summer one man after another had gone deaf and blind and mad with hunger, knew that young fellows who should be out kicking football, shifting girls in discos, making love, building homes and families, were sitting naked in bare rooms repeating other people's slogans, smearing and choking their minds with the left-over excrement of History – she allowed her mother's letter to speak to her only of the peace of small rocky fields, turf-bog spread lazily at their feet, child's drawing of mountain lying across the horizon, the neighbours so good with lifts and shopping and sure we'll meet you at the airport. The rope had twitched again pulling her back and, anaesthetised with gratitude, she asked no questions, let herself be pulled.

Driving down from the airport she had been warmed by the remembered prettiness of hill and hedgerow and old grey monastery, impressed by the new prosperity of bright little bungalows with white rail fences. "Like a returned Yank!" Tim sneered, drawing her attention instead to the posters and the scrawled slogans, a photo of Mrs Thatcher with the caption: *This Woman is a Mass Murderer. Do not attempt to apprehend her yourself: Call on the Provisional IRA.*

"Witty!" Helen said, and Tim looked at her in unbelieving disgust.

Their mother, trying to make peace between them, had spoken of the Pope's visit, the great boost it had been for the morale of the country. "I never thought I'd live to see our Holy Father here in Ireland, though indeed what country has a better right to welcome him after the centuries of martyrdom we endured for our Faith."

"Then it's a pity he didn't come to the part needed him most," Tim said. "He made damn sure he didn't venture too far north. Here listen to this one, Helen: big broad clergyman, big broad Ballymena accent, 'A'm tallin' yez, brethren, if they let thon lad across the border he'll not be kissin the groun', he'll be bitin' the dust!'" Helen was on tenterhooks; in the past an irreverence like that would have earned him the flat of a hand across his jaw, but their mother didn't seem to notice, turned away with a vague smile to point out some big new tourist hotel. I suppose she's mellowing, Helen had thought at the time, she's getting on after all ...

... A noise that she knew from the telly was the sound of a muffled explosion growled through the night, rattled the windows, lingered casually grumbling between the walls for a while, became part of the dark. "There's the

Barrack away up in smoke!" her mother said flippantly as though she had never been asleep. Helen had a mad and desolate vision of floodlit bodies being hurtled mercilessly towards the stars (tell us, Mister Einstein luv, how long is an instant when you're being blown apart?).

"Oh do you think ... " half rising from her chair with a helpful St John's Ambulance face.

"N-o-o-t at all child, troth and you'd know all right if it was the Barrack, you wouldn't be sitting there so cool. It was the wrong direction anyhow, I'd say that was somewhere up the Dundalk road, some old patrol or another. We'll hear the hellys in a minute taking off to investigate." They did. "Some poor mothers' sons for all that," she mourned, atoning for the flippancy and Helen said, because there was nothing to say, "I'm afraid I let the fire die down. Will I get you a cardigan?"

"If you wouldn't mind," she said, "the old Aran in the wardrobe and I'll make us a wee cup of tea and a biscuit."

Helen checked that Caroline had not been woken then went to her mother's room, stumbling across the sheepskin rug to draw the curtains before she put the light on because the night before two blackened faces had leered in at her, pressed up against the pane. They lay up in the ditches all night, her mother said, or in some cattle shelter in the corner of the field and were picked up by helicopter in the early morning. Whatever they expected to find in a retired widow's flowerbeds ... Must be unnerving, she thought, alone here night after night and me in a foreign country and Tim living miles away. She knew that was the whole problem. She had known it even while she raged at her mother asleep and remote from her. It's not me she's shutting out at all, she thought, it's them out there, and the screeches of the random dead, and all the heroes and the villains and the sly boys lining their pockets and every poor fool that ever dreamed of lying up in a tri-coloured coffin clasping a bunch of lilies in his stainless marble hand. And could you blame her?

A neighbour fellow got taken from his house a while back, was jostled into a stolen car, tried by a People's Court and executed – his unfortunate corpse boobytrapped left lying in the road like an abandoned car waiting for some poor cod of a paramedic trooper to try taking his pulse. An informer. The green green grass of home, Tim called him and even that didn't earn him a clout on the gob. They were at school with him, Helen and Tim both and *she* taught him. He'd have been part of the line-up reciting Pearse. She recalled him as a bit of a slabber, knew it all, all the ins and outs, all the local gossip. An informer though? Walking self-righteously straight-backed up to ring the Barrack doorbell or whispering secrets to some slimy blackguard in the corner of a pub? Hard to imagine but then who can you trust these days? That's what she must be thinking, or not thinking, floating into sleep, spending her well-known Christian charity on the griefs of some actress or another, you knew where you were with the telly and the love stories, they wouldn't turn round and repeat some innocent peevish remark to the boys. And the handsome blue-chinned hero wouldn't ever turn out to be Captain Nairac looking for news.

Her things were hanging up neatly in the wardrobe: coats, jackets, dresses. And there in the middle of them, cleaned and pressed and well looked-after was the grey flannel coat Helen had bought her in Paris thirteen years earlier. It was the same one all right, silk label discreetly flaunting itself. If she'd thought about it at all Helen would have expected it to be thrown out years ago, slashed to rags, given to some gypsy at the very least. Her mother's rages used to be like that: destroy the better to forgive. Helen was gathered up and wrung breathless in the grip of an instant's hate, image following merciless image of half-buried injustices, tyranny, intolerance, then she relaxed and stretched herself deliberately in the warmth of other memories.

To think that she kept the coat, cared for it, obviously wore it from time to time! There was a scarf twisted round the neck, not a great match, she'd buy her another when they went to Newry tomorrow, blue-grey silk, gentle and undramatic as the sky over Slieve Gullion. They'd go here and there sightseeing and they'd eat in one of the big tourist hotels; she used to thrive on that sort of outing years ago. Helen recalled the day her mother came tearing up to Belfast intent on murder and instead they went to dine in the Pig 'n' Chicken and Helen forced her to eat asparagus because it was the dearest vegetable on the menu and she came out in a rash that disfigured her for weeks. She never let on she was allergic to it because Helen was treating her and because she was feeling guilty at having listened to backbiting gossip about her daughter.

Helen was nineteen then, working in the Civil Service after being expelled from teacher training college for going to London with a Protestant student to take part in an Africa Freedom march, and they'd told her mother, someone had written to her, some jealous cow, that Helen was still going around with the Prod and attending Socialist meetings and everything, and she went in a terrible state to Belfast, fully intending to pull the hair out of her daughter's head and boot her down home like some Edna O'Brien heroine in front of the countryside. Only the landlady talked to her for an hour before Helen got in from work and assured her that there wasn't one word of truth in the report, that she was a good-living wee girl well settled down now after the shaking-up she got, going to her religious duties regular and running up to St Teresa's Hall every Sunday night like all the rest to dance with nice Catholic boys from Andersonstown and in no time at all she'd be married to some schoolteacher or bank man and before Mrs McCabe knew where she was she'd be nursing a clatter of grandchildren aye missus ah'm tallin' ye! So instead of a row they went to see Doreen Hepburn in the Arts Theatre and Helen took her out to dinner in a posh restaurant and everything was easy and friendly. Except that her mother came out in a rash. And, because she'd kept the coat Helen felt that things would be easier now too, the distance that separated them would go, they'd be able to talk together the way they used to. In spite of the years of silence she'd kept it, she'd worn it, that was surely some indication of her state of mind, of the affection there still was between them.

Four years after the Belfast episode Helen was married and separated, working in Paris, her husband left behind in London. "No reconciliation is possible, Mammy," she wrote. "Don't even suggest I go back to that man!" Her mother went flying over, one hand full of Mass Bouquets for her intentions, the other raised ready to batter her back to respectability. Helen said she was well battered already, threw off her clothes to show the scars and the half-faded bruises, said she'd stuck a whole year of that and Sacrament or no Sacrament she had no intention of going back. By that time her mother was crying over her and saying: "Well the blaggard! Well I always said he was nothing only a pup! Well the jumped-up beggar's get, I'll settle him for good and all!" When she stopped crying and calmed down she said Helen was perfectly right and wasn't it a sensible decision to leave London, he'd never think of looking for her across the Channel. Helen said there was no danger of him sending out search parties, he was fixed up already, no shortage of willing ladies in swinging London and no doubt as soon as the divorce went through he'd get to work on some other poor innocent. Her mother said a divorce wouldn't be much advantage to Helen and was she sure the marriage had been consummated properly because if not they could start applying straight away for an annulment. Helen asked wouldn't the scars do and her mother said no, violence was considered a natural hazard of marriage but any inability to perform his duties would be a different matter entirely. Helen said it was consummated all right but thanks be to God she wasn't pregnant or anything. Her mother said indeed it was nothing to be thankful for, it was a terrible pity because she had a long lonely life before her now and what a mistake it was to rush foolishly into marriage like that and unless he died young Helen had forfeited any chance of having a home of her own and children.

"But," she said, "you can always count on me in any problems or difficulties, I'll always be there and you have a good home waiting for you whenever you need it. Though," she added, "it might be best not to go back to Ireland yet awhile with the sort of nosy neighbours we have, it'd do old Feeney's heart good to see you in the middle of another scandal!"

Helen hadn't wanted to go home then anyway. She was free and the world was wide. She was so relieved at her mother's attitude and to tell the truth so happy at seeing her that she rushed her off to a famous boutique where they were having a sale and found her this lovely grey coat and spent the two months' wages on it that she'd saved up to go to Cuba with. Her mother loved the coat and never stopped talking about the cut of it and the simplicity and it was the nicest thing she ever owned and nothing would do her but to rig Helen out from the same shop, she was a holy show with the face of some hooligan pop star plastered across her chest, a married woman in a tragic situation it was neither right nor proper to be dolling herself up like a teenager.

Helen told her it was no pop star, that was Che

Guevara she said, it was the face of a saint Mammy, a real saint, they were after killing him in Bolivia fighting for the cause of the poor and the oppressed and couldn't she see it wasn't a pop star, pop singers didn't look like that, the dedication, the nobility and didn't her mother think he looked more like a sort of Jesus Christ I mean the way Jesus probably did look Mammy not the awful holy pictures and her mother drew back and would have lifted her hand to her only she remembered in time they were in public. She said don't ever say a thing like that Helen not even in a joke, Our Blessed Lord was wise and gentle and peaceful at all times and killed or no killed yon thing was more like some of the heroes you'd see propping up Murphy's corner on a Dole day.

Helen told her every single person in Paris, my God, Mammy, even old people like Yves Montand and Sartre, venerated this guy and everyone was wearing his face on their sweater and quoting from his book every single person Mammy, and the crowds surged in and out of the boutique with his face on their bags and scarves humming 'Duerme Negrito' and 'Changuito Guerrillero', and her mother laughed and said oh my a my the latest from Paris, you were always the great one for following fashion! Helen tried to explain that she was changed, that she was more mature now and it wasn't just fashion, fashion had nothing got to do with it, the way people everywhere were changing their natures because of the example of this one fab human being and soon there'd be a whole new race of mankind wise and compassionate and brave who'd be ready to drop everything, he was a doctor Mammy imagine a qualified doctor, and go off to fight injustice anywhere in the world.

And her mother said Helen was to be sure and send her a postcard when that happened and new man or no new man he still looked like some cornerboy. They had a bitter argument there in the shop, Helen trying to convince her, and her mother said she was making a show of herself in front of the people and to come on out for heavens sake.

All the same they had a great week, it was the last time they enjoyed themselves together, it was the last time they saw each other till now. In the end she went home in the lovely coat saying her daughter's happiness would always be the first intention in her prayers and that she was glad anyway Helen was fitted up with a good decent job and please God she'd make some suitable friends and above all she was to keep pure and good and resist temptation. As an Irish Catholic she was in a special position and had a duty to set an example to everyone she came across. She shoved a wad of Novena leaflets into Helen's pocket and the address of a Legion of Mary group that she'd got from the concierge, the pair of them having struck up a friendship whose vocabulary consisted of words like Lourdes, Lisieux, Cluny and which, Helen knew, had destroyed any chance of a private life for her, she'd have to move digs. She couldn't stop crying on the coach back from the airport; it came to her that her whole life long, since the evening she got dumped in the Convent, her mother was constantly going home to warmth and shelter and leaving her alone in some horrible place to cope with things. Then she stopped crying and went to give her evening classes at the Berlitz ...

" ... Can you not find it? Sure take any old cardigan and come on, your tea's wet and everything."

She had the fire started up again with a couple of firelighters and a whole heap of briquettes, the waste of it so near bedtime, but lovely and welcoming to take the last bit of chill off Helen's memories. The coffee table with the fancy tiled top was pulled up on the hearthrug with pink marshmallow biscuits and a plate of bread for toasting. It was neat and bright and homely. Helen thought of her own basement flat with its constant smell of damp from the river and its chronic untidiness and all of a sudden she wanted desperately to be let stay, to let her life slide gently, unquestioningly, between teacup and telly, all the neat little truths lined up in order, with Heaven swept and dusted waiting at the end. She wanted more than anything for her mother to say: "Sure I can see you're not happy at all over there and why need you go back when there's a good home waiting for you here." But her mother gave no cue at all and the moment passed, as it always had. Helen commented on the nice cosy sitting-room and her mother said: "But I suppose you have your own flat lovely, you were always a great one for painting and decorating."

Helen, relaxed with the flow of memories, did not reply with the clichés she'd been using ever since she came home but told her mother at length about the big free-and-easy apartment on the Amstel, its doors always open to anyone who needed help or shelter. She said they were trying to live their lives in love and simplicity and tolerance, and told how Caroline from the very day she was born had been encouraged to mix with people of all races and creeds and social levels without the slightest distinction. She described the economy of their lives, how she wove all the curtains herself and knitted or sewed every stitch they wore and how Pieter had retrieved some old dining chairs from the Flea Market and made them like new and how he constructed this massive table out of old beams from a demolished house – they needed a huge table, she said, for they never knew who or how many would descend on them at mealtimes. Her mother smiled and said yes, it sounds lovely, you seem to have no shortage of friends anyway, and then she changed the subject and said well it's getting near bedtime if we want to be up to catch this bus in the morning. Helen helped her to clear away the dishes and they went amicably to bed.

Miss Feeney arrived early next morning to take Caroline for the day and Helen, to hide her dislike of the old spinster, was effusive in her thanks. Miss Feeney looked at her sharply and said she used to put on less airs and graces and what were neighbours for, there was no need to make a ceremony out of it, and many's the time she'd looked after Helen aye and skelped her legs for her many's the time and the old ways were still the best and it was a poor thing indeed when young people grew too far away from the place and the people that reared them.

Well there's one that hasn't changed much, Helen thought, recalling how her mother had never been able to stand old Feeney either, and there they were now, apparently bosom friends, retired on the same day, identical bungalows a few yards apart, never done in and out making wee cups of tea for each other. Suddenly depressed she said: "Ah sure we might as well take Caroline to Newry with us, there'll hardly be any danger," but her mother said no, no it wouldn't be right to take the risk, especially after that ambush last night, two dead, it was on the News this morning, and Miss Feeney said you'd never forgive yourself Helen if anything happened to her and anyway Father Joseph's dying to have a good crack with her, a wee Dutch girl, he was out there you know in some Dutch colony for years and years, so Helen let her go and walked with her mother to catch the bus on the Square.

"Do you never get sick of old Feeney?" she asked, turning from the mountains she hadn't see for fifteen years to the road she hadn't seen either, its grass verges littered with rusty carcasses of burnt-out cars that even the soldiers were no longer fool enough to touch. "Who? What's that?" Her mother had been dozing against the back of the seat and woke with a jerk. "Feeney. She's a bit of an old pain, isn't she? How do you stick her next door?" "Peg Feeney's a good neighbour to me, Helen, and she was a good principal for twenty years as well you know. I have nothing only the highest respect for her and never had." "Go away outa that with you!" Helen laughed. "Sure you were never done complaining about her and making a joke of her as long as I remember, it's news to me she was a good boss to you." "When you get to my age, daughter, maybe you'll see the good of having someone nearby that you can depend on. When a body's own flesh and blood is not at hand – "

To Helen's relief she was interrupted; the bus was halted at a road-block. "The blaggards in green are the worst," her mother whispered, "Oul' RUC men!" Helen wasn't so sure: the young soldiers with their comically disguised faces looked nervous, their eyes skittering dangerously around and over the passengers. The others, the policemen, were older and solider; they might possibly act with thick brutality if they took the notion but were unlikely to fire off a shot out of pure panic. The soldiers took names and addresses. Two of their mates had died horribly the night before. Did they really believe the killers were casually sauntering to market on a quiet country bus? But then maybe they were. Helen gave her address in Amsterdam.

"What are you, a journalist?"

"No, I'm here on holiday."

The officer laughed shortly: "Christ, you must be a masochist! Actually I took the wife and kids to Holland last year. To the Keukenhof, been there?"

The kids and the flower festival and the pert little lacquered wife oohing and aahing over the pink flamingoes. Normality. Sweet suburban decency and he must wonder, every time he put that clown's paint on his face, every time he manned a roadblock, if normality was something he'd seen the last of forever. Helen guessed he was seeing her as some link with a future in which he, lucky survivor, took the proud kids and adoring wife for a nostalgic dander through the tulip fields. She had an impulse to smile, to speak of the smell of hyacinths – because what unavoidable land-mine might he be already headed towards unbeknownst? – but she shook her head, cowardly, refusing friendly contact.

"Weren't they nervous!" she said, back in the bus, "did you notice their eyes?"

"Troth and I never look near them!" her mother answered loudly. "I wouldn't give them that much satisfaction."

A few people nearby murmured swift agreement, because who can you trust these days, and the murmurs caught and spread and rolled from seat to seat, ritual responses in a rosary of hate.

"Isn't it shocking," her mother said when they were installed in a café halfway through the morning, "Do you remember the time people could go here and there as free as they pleased? No roadblocks, no searching your handbag, and you weren't on the verge of a heart-attack every time someone left a parcel behind on a chair. Will it ever end, do you think? The pity of it, all this bombing and killing, God help us all, where will it finish up?"

"I thought you'd have been all in favour of it," Helen said, to punish her for the scene on the bus. "You were always so patriotic. It's a great thing to die for your country, you kept telling us from when we were no size. With Feeney it was die for your faith. You could say we had a choice all right!"

"This wasn't what I meant, nobody ever visualised this, Helen. Honest to God this brutality has little to do with patriotism, there's a difference between idealism and mindless killing, though I'm not saying they haven't a just cause. Only nobody ever recommended such – " Such blood, Helen thought, you imagined one could die for Ireland without blood and without vomit and without squeals, and above all without killing anyone else. A nice white smooth death, lying in one smiling photogenic piece under the green and saffron flag. But she didn't say it because what was the point of needlessly wounding? And her mother was after all just an innocent bystander: essentially good, essentially harmless.

"Did I ever tell you," she asked instead, to lighten the atmosphere, "about the time I tried to join the IRA? Well I was all of fourteen, it was the time Monica Quinn's mother took me and Monica up to Dublin for the weekend and Monica's brother, you know Jimmy, he was on the run for blowing up a Customs hut? Well I sort of saw me as the Countess Markiewicz and him as de Valera. I mean I was convinced he'd get me into the organisation, so Monica fixed up this rendezvous in the Phoenix Park and I went along trying to look about thirty all plastered in orange lipstick that I'd ripped off in Woolworths. So what happens? Along comes this great King Kong type, all beef. I mean I'd never *met* Jimmy before, and before you could say Patrick Pearse, he had me up against a tree and was trying to shove a hairy big paw down my dress! Imagine! So, I mean fourteen in that day and age, girls had a sex-age of about two, so I ran off screaming blue murder. But just think of it Mammy, only for that attempted grope your darling daughter would no doubt be making her own wee contribution to History!"

"No, you never told me," her mother said. "Well, we'd better be getting on. You have your shopping to do and I have a few things to get in the market."

To Helen, walking through the grey town watching ordinary people with ordinary faces like her own smoking in quick nervous puffs up and down the pavement in and out of shops trying on synthetic jeans, buying packets of synthetic soup, their eyes sliding about at the floor, at the door, at the people beside and behind them, it seemed incredible that the danger they feared was real, that they were not dramatising themselves as she had been dramatising herself at fourteen, that the street *could* of a sudden burst open into flames and smoke and ruin, into a screech of disintegrating lives. That it had already done so several times. But it did not do so that day and they arrived home without incident. Miss Feeney brought Caroline back saying she'd been a great wee girl and no trouble at all. She refused the offer of tea and ran off home to cook a meal for Father Joseph who was a great eater.

"Look what I bought you in Newry, Caroline, and here Mammy this is for you, just a wee present."

"Oh Helen you shouldn't have, the lovely scarf, ah sure it's too good to me you are, it's beautiful, Helen!"

"I thought it might go with that grey coat of yours, the one I got you in Paris, I see you still have it."

"Which coat do you ... Oh you mean that old grey thing in the wardrobe? Sure, daughter dear, that thing's in rags years ago! I never wear it now except an odd time I might throw it round my shoulders weeding. But Helen it wasn't you gave me that coat, that was an old one of Peg Feeney's, she gave me a whole lot of things, real good things, when she started to put on weight."

"But Mammy no, the old memory must be going," Helen laughed. "Don't you remember the day we bought it, the awful row we had – I disgraced you in front of all the shopgirls going on about Che Guevara! Sure it has a Paris label and everything, you couldn't mistake it."

"Well I don't remember it at all Helen, I honestly can't recall any row in a shop. Maybe you did buy me a coat, you were always too generous, but it certainly wasn't that one. I don't deny it has a Paris label because Peg bought it the time she went to Lourdes, oh seven years ago and then she got too stout for it and passed it on to me."

Was that true? *Could* it be true and am I going mad, Helen wondered, trying to picture poor old Feeney trotting into the Saint Laurent boutique with her plastic shopping bag. There must surely be some mistake? But her mother was adamant – she could not remember Helen buying her a coat in Paris. She didn't need to throw it away, Helen thought bitterly, beginning to have an inkling. She threw me away instead, she just forgot about me for seven years, replaced me with old Feeney.

Then Caroline chimed in: "Mum, do you know what Miss Feeney's brother did when you were in Newry? He washed my hair for me so he did."

"What? What are you talking about? Washed your hair – of course he didn't wash your hair, stop telling fibs darling!" Everything's gone quite crazy, she thought with a giggle, seeing a tabloid headline: "*Elderly Priest Washes Little Girl's Hair.*"

"But he did Mum honest! He poured water on my hair and he said a recitation and he forgot the shampoo. And then Miss Feeney gave me sweets and she taught me the Name of the Father and the Angel of God. Look Mum, want to see me do the Name of the Father for you?"

Helen understood. She turned on her mother in a fury. "Do you hear that? She's away in the head your bloody old crony, she's halfway round the twist! And that creepy brother of hers, do you realise what they did? Fanatics, religious maniacs, my God, sure that's what they used to accuse old Paisley of long ago, inveigling children to his house to proselytise them. Christ mother I won't put up with this, I'll destroy the pair of them, I'll drag them through every court in the country, I'll – "

Her mother was standing there stiffly in front of her, as she had often stood stiffly and silently in front of an unruly class, wearing an expression Helen remembered all too well. They had jokes about it years ago – Helen used to say: Early Christian waiting for the cage to open. And Tim: Teetotaller about to refuse a drink at a Hunt Ball. Defiant and proud and brave, and slightly self-conscious.

"You knew about it mother, you put them up to it. How dare you, what right – "

"What right, what right! Hadn't I every right? My only daughter living like a slut with a man she's not married to, my only grandchild reared like a heathen. If you heard yourself, if you only heard yourself last night bumming and blowing out of you about the godless life you were leading, mixed up with drug addicts and communists and God knows what, letting your innocent child be corrupted by hooligans, ignorant trash of all creeds and colours. Did you expect me to sit up and do nothing? What class of a mother are you? Bragging to my face about how you stole from Woolworths when I was half-killing myself to give you a good education and the best of everything. You weren't worth my trouble, Helen, and that's something I found out long ago. I gave you every chance to mend your ways but you decided to go your own road. Well so be it, you made your choice, but don't expect me to stand by and do nothing when I see my only grandchild headed straight for Hell!"

And I thought she was changed, I thought she was harmless – seeing the straight simplicity of her mother's life, the ten commandments where they always were, eternal fire waiting for you if you broke them. She had a vision of what her own life must look like in comparison and for an insane second she wanted to fling herself in her mother's arms, cry: "All right, all right I'll make a Catholic of her, I'll send her to Mass, I'll come home, I'll do anything you want!"

Instead she said coldly: "Surely you mean Limbo, mother?" and went to her room to pack.

Tim drove her to Dublin early next morning: "What possessed you to come crawling back? What were you expecting – the maternal lap shaken out of its mothballs for you, roses in the garden and your teddy bear waiting on the pillow? You're a bigger innocent than I thought!"

"Why did she send for me? She did send for me, Tim, was it just to have Caroline baptised?"

"Oh she thought she'd get you to stay, she's dead lonesome you know. After seven years she thought you'd have had enough of a life of sin and be ready to settle down and breathe the saintly air of Cross again. The savour of iniquity cloyeth on the tongue my dear brethren. Only you were no sooner arrived than it was Pieter this and Pieter that and the flat and the friends and the bloody windmills or whatever. She saw she hadn't a chance. You didn't seriously imagine she was going to approve of you?"

"I thought she was changed, I dunno, slacker about things. But she *can't* have expected me to stay celibate, Christ I was only twenty-three when I split up with John!"

"And how old do you think *she* was when Daddy died? Do you think she ever looked at another man?"

"You disapprove too, don't you? You think I shouldn't have got married again?"

"Sure what do I care? You can't seriously believe your prolonged bout of adultery, or whatever you like to call it, is of any interest to anyone? In the light of all *this*?"

She followed his glance to the street of the border village they were driving through, its walls plastered with hand-written posters: DEATH TO TRAITORS! THATCHER OUT! KILL THE BRITS! Smudgy black photographs nailed to trees. Nothing had changed. Nothing ever would. She thought of her mother's letter and its nostalgic image of friendly fields, haws ripening on the bushes. What foolishness had possessed her, to return to this sick place? The hedges were black already, the leaves fallen, you could see the wind slashing wickedly across the famous landscape. Slane, Tara, an old grey monastery. Bogholes rich with the corpses of Cromwell's victims, preserved whole and intact after three centuries. Carrion scawl-crows sitting on posts waiting to gorge themselves on death and desolation. Big black crows rising off bare fences with a sudden meaningless shout of anger or boredom, flapping away aimlessly against the shabby sky. Black flags nailed grimly to tree-trunks: Pray for the soul of Bobby Sands. Pray for the soul of Raymond McCreesh. Pray for the soul of ... Death was everywhere, it was in everything, and life was the unforgivable sin.

"There's places," she said, with an impulse of charity towards this countryside she loved and hated and would not see again, "I've lived in places where they think they can solve any problem under the sun by opening a mail-order catalogue or ringing up the relevant branch of the Social Security; do you think that's any better?"

"I do indeed," he said seriously. "I think it's a hell of a lot better. Wouldn't anyone in their senses?"

Things Fall Apart

Flanagan the master-builder created a thriving small city, set a pub on a quiet street corner, furnished it in bog-oak and formica, hung it with engravings of Emer and Queen Maeve in swooning tones of silver-bronze, and added as an afterthought a western-style swing door and the poster of a local rock group. Flanagan the god created Owen Farrow, patriot, and caused him to reject with holy fervour the proposal of a foreign journalist that between them they could coin a fortune out of sending old Houlihan's daughter, the lovely Kathleen, out to hustle for them on the streets of the world. "You've come to the wrong man," Owen Farrow was saying. "If it's dirty business like that you're after Capella's the boyo for you, go on over there and ask Capella to do your pimping for you!"

"Eh ... who?" the journalist asked warily; a non-Catholic himself he was suspicious of Italian names in this part of the world.

"Arrah man, would you look over yonder, sure everyone knows Capella. The big folk singer sure."

"Ah, a singer." Relieved, the reporter wiped the pair of misty preconceptions he wore instead of glasses and peered through them at the only other occupant of the bar.

"You mean the little leprechaun chappie in bainin breeches and an Aran sweater being sick into a pint of Guinness?"

Pius A Capella, committed poet ('Who weeps now for Vietnam?', 'In Soweto's bored black jungle'), was in fact wearing jeans and an ancient UCLA T-shirt and sipping a glass of tequila but Farrow didn't think it worth coming to blows over. "That's him, that's yer boyo. Make money out of annathin, Pius would!"

And then Flanagan the man, slight and foxy, woken to reality by the rattle of a letter-box two floors down, re-read the six pages he'd typed, found them good, and hooked them into a loose-leaf file labelled: 'Chats in the Chapel – a novel about Irish History.'

Downstairs leered a birthday card from his married sister in Birmingham: 'Did you hit forty or did *it* hit *you?*' and a too-thick brown envelope self-addressed to Ms Jane Flanagan 12 Brondesbury Heights. No promise there, he knew, of an immediate hundred quid; the bitch Paula had written: ' ... rather too crotchety and pessimistic this one, don't you think? However, if you *could* slip in a few of your usual neat puns and perhaps a wee note of hope in the final paragraph, I'd be willing to reconsider it for Her World.' And good holy Christ, Flanagan thought, *they* want equality. Get back to your knitting patterns, Paula, he screamed quietly, puns and sentiment and happy endings yet in a true-life interview with an inner-city single parent, unemployed and worn to a marrowless bone trying to bring up four kids in B & B accommodation! Get back to yer Home Hints, Paula, get back to yer recipes for rock buns!

He shuffled through the other tenants' post (what looked like another Final Reminder for the Ryans, something in a plain brown wrapper for the Whippet, a postcard from Lourdes for Miss Dolan), and imagined a cartoon bubble with himself inside tipping a bottle of acid scorn onto the face of a captive beseeching Woman Editor. Screw Paula, he thought, and wished for a minute he could. A Fleet Street lady would be an achievement, would take some shifting, would be balm for wounds. Only Flanagan would never meet Paula, knew no one who could get him asked to the sort of party a female mag editor would attend. Neat gin and pickled gherkins probably, in some tarted-up Islington slum, he thought, picturing Paula's sour little smile on Page One. And even invited to such a party, Flanagan the man would not exist, Paula would never be introduced to the sexy author of those witty little monthly articles. For the sake of the dropping shilling Flanagan had castrated himself: in Paula's eyes (and occasionally in his own) he existed only as Miz Jane, a sort of Southern belle-wether whom she paid to write perceptive pieces on the plight of captive wives in big cities. With a note of hope in the final paragraph. Aw screw Paula, he thought again, she could whistle for her puns.

Flanagan, up at five-thirty to work on 'Chats', wanted his breakfast. He went down the basement stairs and stood well back in the corner by the telephone, outside big Josie's door. From that spot you could hear everything that went on in the house – he listened now to the scringe of bedsprings as the old landlady shook herself awake and reached for her false teeth, to Eileen Foley skelping Carmel, to the Ryans having an early morning go at each other, to poor Miss Dolan scampering fearfully past the Whippet's door on her way to the bathroom.

On the evening he moved in, six months earlier, Flanagan was standing legitimately enough in that corner going through the Yellow Pages when he heard a peevish male voice (surely familiar?) bleating: "If you did a bit of housework now and then you mightn't feel so bloody frustrated and unfulfilled!" There was an explosion of crockery against walls and, two minutes later, hurled by some mighty invisible arm, a small pale Social Security Inspector well known to Flanagan landed at his feet, said "Oops, sorry!", picked himself up and scuttled off like the White Rabbit, followed by a Sainsbury's carrier-bag spilling off-white linen and with it a voice that shook the building, threw open twelve flat doors and knocked 'The Gleaners' off Miss Dolan's wall: "Don't forget yer woy-frunce, Cyril!"

The young man was already gone, leaving a trail of good-quality underwear (which Joe Ryan collected and gave to his wife to wash). "And begod that's the last time I shack up with a feckin English dole-man!"

Flanagan, cringing away before the mass of enraged female muscle it would take to send a Civil Servant and his belongings flying like saucers in a tenement corridor, looked up through spread fingers and saw, leaning on the door-jamb, plumply grinning, hands on hips, sleeves thrust up, his old friend Janey Quinn from home. Only it couldn't be Janey, Janey was married this twenty years with a family, this must be her eldest, Josie, the one that went away to England.

Josie made much of him; there was a lot of "Oul' times!" which Flanagan found unnecessary and distasteful. Josie was what he usually kept well away from in London – the famine-ship mentality that tended to creep in whenever two exiles met ('Are y'over long?' 'Six months.' 'I suppose yer thinkin it's six munce too many!'). He could swear Janey Quinn was on her knees at home every night saying the Prayer for Emigrants after the Rosary. But big Josie, whether he liked it or not, adopted him like a stray kitten into her big guffawing amoral life. And big Josie was handy. He might in the depths of himself, shake a fastidious puritanical head over this example of today's teenagers, but big Josie fed him and listened to him and confided to him useful bits of womanly information that he jotted down and slid casually into his articles.

After ten minutes outside her door without hearing a man's voice or a cleared throat or the buzz of a razor, he decided he was in luck for breakfast. The flat was full of a good morning whiff of bacon. "I see you got something back," Josie said, "Was it that interview with poor Sheila?"

"Yeah, the bitch wants puns. Puns, I ask you!"

"I'd a thought there was no better man. Heard you hard at it in the wee small hours, could you not fit a silencer on that feckin typewriter? Look!" she went on, "Look what I got in the post! They want me in three weeks, isn't it fantastic?"

"Who wants you?"

"That family. *You* know. That mother's help job in France I applied for."

"You're not going, are you? I never thought you were serious, Jesus you're out of your mind Josie. Throwing up a good soft job in the Civil Service in this day and age, what'll you do when you get back, what'll you live on?"

"Who mentioned coming back, I'm not even away yet! Look I'm nineteen Jamesy, you don't think I'm going to spend me whole life chatting up Harlesden's share of the three million, do ye? I want to see a bit of the world before I'm past it. God yer a right old woman all the same Flanagan, yer as bad as me ma!"

He looked at her, big and untidy, slummocking round the flat making the breakfast in a mauve nylon dressing-gown and worn-down fur mules, and he found it hard to imagine her strolling down the Champs Elysées.

"You'll never survive it," he said. "You don't know what that lot's like, make mincemeat out of you!"

(Flanagan realised he was full of a desolate emptiness and hastily converted it into concerned pity: Mother's help my foot, they'd have her scrubbing floors till she dropped, a good-natured big lump like that.) "Poor old Jos," he said, "I can't really see you making it in Gay Paree!"

"It's Gay Lyons actually. Hey!" she said, "there's a new one for your Rogues Gallery, listen: This is RTE with our special reporter Gay Lyons covering the local scene. Sad demise of Owen Farrow at the hands, or rather teeth, of the old sow he was vowed to save!" She imitated the breathless tones of a TV announcer on to a scoop. Flanagan absentmindedly considered the idea and then realised she was laughing at him. "Why don't you write something yourself," he snarled, "if you're all that smart?"

"Scared stiff of our ones," she answered seriously enough. "Whatever I wrote about they'd swear was after happening to me in the back of a car coming back from a disco. But just you wait Flanagan, when I'm fat and forty with a houseful of kids I'll start sending wee stories to the magazines. Interior monologues and everything."

She didn't *seem* to be joking, though you never knew with big Josie. Maybe (shoved away probably in the back of a drawer full of laddered tights, and ready to be forced on him for appreciation) there existed a school exercise book full of fraught little short stories about a sensitive adolescent's loss of innocence. You never could tell with people: look at poor Briggs at school, the very spit of a beer-swilling English philistine and yet there he was, week after week, hopefully groping up Culture's skirts, doing New Statesman competitions for all he was worth. Parodies of everyone from Rabelais to Karol Wojtyla.

"I'm forty today," he said, to ward off disclosures.

"Well y'are and a few more, sure you were at school with me mother!"

"I wasn't *at* school with her," he snapped, "She *took* me to school. By the hand. I was in Infants the year she went away to the Convent."

"Oh well never mind," she soothed, "You don't look it

anyway. And now, it's not that I'm chasing you out or anything but I have to put on me clothes and get out to me work. Are you not going in to school today?"

"They don't need me till eleven."

"Oh great! You can be an angel and do me a favour then. I have this fella coming for a meal tonight and I heard a gorgeous recipe for avocado pears on telly. Only they have to be chilled for about six hours so I thought if you'd nip up the greengrocers for me you could shove a dollop of shrimp in the middles and just bung them in the fridge, do you mind?" She handed him a jar of sandwich filling and he laughed: "You're slipping Josie. The way to a man's heart, or wherever, is definitely *not* through fishpaste avocados!"

"Oh I'm getting a chicken and chips as well, from the take-away. And lychees."

"You better promise me the leavings then," he teased, "or I swear I'll be down listening outside your door."

"Aye, yourself and the Whippet. The pair of you should form an old bachelors' co-operative."

He laughed but went back upstairs angry and depressed. He'd meant to do some more work on 'Chats' but was now superstitiously afraid to take it out of its folder in case it had fallen flat on him during breakfast. He thought gloomily about it, cursed himself for wasting time with big Josie, then lit a cigarette and began picking possible winners out of last night's Standard, his usual Yankee to give him an aim in getting through till four o'clock, a small insane hope that could be trusted to wink at him now and again through the long dismal hours with Remedial B. A couple of sturdy outsiders, eights, tens, for possible treasure-trove and fill in with a solid base of money-ons to cover himself.

Feeling slightly better he put a cupful of water in a saucepan on the gas ring, opened a jar of Nescafé.

Elegance, would he ever know style? To lead a lovely wayfaring woman with a Linda Loring face to the deep leather couch before a chimney-full of blazing logs. A little nachtmusick on the stereo, amber liquid in a crystal glass ... aw would you quit it! All the same, even big Josie's flat when she left ... No, the old bag downstairs would grab her chance to double the rent. If he found a publisher for 'Chats' he'd be able to move. To give up teaching. He drank his coffee. Old Houlihan's daughter, the lovely Kathleen, sat in a corner of the pub weeping over her wounds, telling the endless tale of her ravishment. Her listeners were themselves wounded – more or less seriously, more or less crippled and maimed, more or less on the point of death – but Miss Houlihan, unaware, forced on their attention the (admittedly deep) cut on her own head, and told once more in beautiful lamenting tones the tale of her woes. A bit too obvious maybe. And time to get out to school: half past ten, the day already sliding inevitably towards bathos ...

" ... Well I could have bitten my tongue out the minute I said it. Kindly address me as Sir, I told him, and would you mind removing your hands from your pockets when you're addressing a teacher. Well it was just one of those daft reflexes, throwback to my own old days with the Christian Brothers. You know."

They didn't know. Flanagan realised they had no idea what he was talking about, Christian Brothers were outside their experience. *They* had known only the matiness of the Froebel-trained (pretend you're a tree, let it all hang out, teacher's a pal and spit in me eye for creative expression). He admitted sadly that no communication was possible between him and these child-faced graduates and moved away to where Jenny Lane, officer's daughter hitting thirty and more his target, was breathlessly describing the conversion of a bankrupt factory into a high-tech squatters' paradise: "Forty-foot ceilings, the heaven of it! So Simon got busy on the filing-cabinets with this fantastic peacock-blue lacquer while I ... "

Flanagan was interested, angled for an invitation to join the do-it-yourself block of flats. "I'm looking for a pad actually," he began. She considered him out of gymkhana-girl eyes under a straight hazel fringe. "Yes," she said with flat dismissive sympathy, "It must be difficult for a single man on his own. Have you thought of asking in the shops around here? They sometimes know of digs ... "

She thinks I'm ninety, she thinks I'm the Whippet. And he sat, suddenly shrunken, ignored in the vinyl armchair, age loitering at his back waiting to grab him by the shoulders and shake him hairless, toothless, cockless, a single man on his own in a single room, warming up the Horlicks on a single gas burner ...

"Ooh *there* you are Mr Flanagan! My elusive colleague! I come, as you see, bearing gifts, just a teeny tiny poetry book you might care to use with your Remedials. I often think we don't offer them enough *Beauty* don't you agree Mr Flanagan? All these squalid little picture books about back street vandals written in words of one syllable ... Just because they're backward readers doesn't mean ... "

"'Fraid one syllable's all my lot know, Miss Saunders. To judge by their conversation."

"Ooh now Mr Flanagan, mustn't be cynical must we? Poor little dears. Have you had a look round the district yet? Rough diamonds of course, what can one expect, but I do sincerely feel that if we take the trouble to dig deep enough we'll reach ore in the end don't you agree Mr Fla ... "

Ore yourself, he thought, trying to shut out the refined coo that kept on rubbing away like sandpaper in the depths of his ear. High-cheeked maidens from Tir na nÓg soothed his brow, caressed his body, restored him to manhood.

" ... so I thought Mr Flanagan if you've nothing more wildly exciting of course ... just French bread and cheese you know and, you'll be glad to hear, some *very* good sherry ... " He drove a wooden stake through her heart, buried her in quicklime. A lovely woman with swooning eyes led him by the hand to a secret mountain hide-out ...

Ostentatiously he opened his folder, began making notes for the next chapter of his book. Still in a corner of the pub and well launched now, Kathleen Ní Houlihan was describing with age-old bitterness the tyrannical master who was forever holding her in subjection. With the exception of Owen Farrow (drowning in the mists of her long dim hair) and Pius A Capella (fishing for lost causes in the depths of his glass), her audience was beginning to fidget and look puzzled – they knew that the yeoman captain who'd raped Kathleen long ago, far from being fit to quell anyone with fiery glare, was limping around with one foot in the grave and the other in a puddle of North Sea oil, feebly dragging a wasted self-abused carcase through the marketplaces of Europe, Britannia still gamely trying to waive the rules ...

"Och there y'are Paddy me ould shillelagh! Would yous be after givin me now the benefit of yer vast erudition? I meantersay old chappie what what! Sorry Miss Saunders, I'm about to kidnap your demon lover, duty calls and all that. And in return for that valiant rescue," Briggs continued, making for two vacant chairs, "I badly need the assistance of your literary talents."

"What's it this week?"

"Poet Laureate brain-drained to the States writing an ode on the Gulf War. Only I'm missing one teeny tiny syllable, as dear Saunders would put it. Here, have an eyeful."

You're missing more than a syllable, Flanagan thought, reading: 'Gaily down the Oval Office/Trips a six-gun-toting ... '. The bell rang for class.

"It's Ted Hughes these days actually," he said, "but why don't we thrash it out over a few jars this evening, you could pick me up about eight, OK?"

"Fine," Briggs said. "Then you can introduce me to the tart with the 'eart. Has she, uh, lepped on you yet?"

"No fear, she as good as told me I was old enough to be her father!"

"I'd pay no heed to that, old son, just give her a huge nudge and see what happens. Might be the making of you! I don't want to butt in but ... "

"No, don't butt in!" Flanagan said sharply, feeling that his prolonged celibacy was no concern of the Deputy Head, and then: "Sorry, I mean ... "

"Not to worry Paddy, not to worry," leading the way towards the classroom block and adding in a different tone: "Listen old chap, MacKenzie was telling me you had a spot of aggro with him this morning. Some nonsense about calling you Sir? He seemed rather put-out. Think you could smooth things over? I see you're down to take them again this afternoon. It *is* rather important Paddy, as you'll see when you've been here as long as the rest of us. Do what you can old chap, right?"

"Christ!" Flanagan moaned theatrically, "That it should come to this! The noble profession! A good Honours degree forced to lick the boots of a shower of half-witted cretins and they call that teaching! All right, Briggs, *all* right, I'll see what I can do."

And stop calling me Paddy, he snarled silently.

"It's a touchy district," Briggs said. "Hundred per cent mixed, ninety per cent unemployed. Got to wear gloves on the job, old chap. MacKenzie's their big boss-man: with him on your side you might just win through. Otherwise ... well Soweto's not in it, believe you me!"

An hour later Flanagan was lingering in the bog over a

last neurotic smoke before he faced Remedial B. He tried to ironise the situation into importance, tried to cast himself as the heroine of a 'Her World' serial: 'Will MacKenzie be able to forgive and forget? Don't miss our next gripping instalment!'

Walking down the long corridor he tried to picture Spencer Churchill MacKenzie through the eyes of a sympathic social worker – bright, handsome, a born leader, fruit of a broken home and a broken street where barricades tended to sprout up spontaneously at the mere footfall of a constable on the beat. A sophisticated telly vocabulary and impressive store of general knowledge, though unable to read at fifteen and a half – but then with nothing more demanding in his future to read than a Benefit form ... Poor wee bugger all the same, Flanagan thought, when he leaves here in six months he'll be flung on the scrap-heap with the rest of them. But he knew the easy sympathy would go at the first ironic glance from MacKenzie in the front desk, egging him on, waiting for him to crack up like the poor sod whose place Flanagan was filling. Passing the door of Remedial A, he heard Miss Saunders reciting, with the hysterical enthusiasm he assumed came from four decades of keeping herself pure for Mr Right: 'Ooh what a commotion under the ground/When March cries Hoo there Hoo!'

He braced himself for the chaos that would flap dark noisy wings in his face when he opened the Pandora's box of Remedial B.

To his uneasy amazement the class was standing orderly and silent in four rows, hands in pockets, MacKenzie facing them like a sergeant-major, holding the blackboard pointer. "Shun! Att-ten-SHUN!" he bawled as Flanagan came in: "Hands OUT!" Sixty hands whipped out of pockets, held themselves up for inspection, thirty faces mimed craven terror, thirty voices sobbed: "Sorry surr!

Things Fall Apart

Surry sorr! Wasn't doing nothing nasty I wasn't surr! You can check sorr, if you like surr!"

"Oh come off it!" Flanagan snapped. "Get to your places all of you." They didn't move. "See man, you hurt their feelings," MacKenzie said gently. "You gotta talk nice to them surr. What you gotta say is: 'And now ladies and gentlemen would you mind taking your seats.' Only manners, sir, innit? You get a big buzz outa manners don't you surr? So you scratch our backs, we scratch yours, get it man?" Flanagan got it. He bowed ironically and invited them to be seated. "And what's it to be today sorr?"

"Wanna discuss a ... fillum, surr?" "No, tell us an Irish joke sorr." "Yeah, the wan about the mounkey and the dounkey!" "Or we could draw a map of de British Oils? Surr?"

"Listen here boy, when you learn how to speak the Queen's English yourself, you'll have earned the right to mimic mine."

"Ooh la la, the Queen's English!" warbled a falsetto voice from the back, "Gay days we're having, sorr!"

Ramesh Patel danced down the aisle wiggling his hips, waving his wrist limply. The class exploded.

"Silence!" Flanagan roared. "Can't you, just once, try to behave like sane normal human beings?"

Concepta O'Keeffe jumped on a desk and began removing her tights: "Oh I'm normal surr, c'mere and see how normal I am!"

At a signal from MacKenzie the boys leaped to their feet and sank their hands in their pockets, jumping up and down as if in agony. Flanagan realised that the whole performance was carefully organised, had probably been rehearsed several times since his tactless remark to MacKenzie before lunch.

Attempting to fight down the shrill humiliation of rage he decided to talk sense to them on their own terms: "Now listen here kids, let's be reasonable eh? Believe you me I wouldn't be here either except I've got a living to earn. *I'm* not the big bad wolf who's keeping you at school till you're sixteen. But if you had any wit in your thick skulls you'd realise that this here is the cushiest spot you'll ever be in, in your whole miserable wee lives. What do you want: nursemaids? You'd like me to spoonfeed you, tuck you in and say your prayers for you? Well take it from me, lads, in a few months time you'll be out there on your knees licking the arse of some fat factory manager begging a job. *If* there are any factories left by then. If they haven't all been painted peacock blue by some snooty tart that thinks she's the Princess of Wales. Or else you'll be signing up in Harlesden every week with thousands more like you. And nobody'll give a fuck whether you can read and write or whether your mum dropped you on your head when you were a pup. If you lot realised what … "

"Yous wans, man!"

"What was that, MacKenzie?"

"You referred to us as 'you lot', surr, and I was just putting you right. To be ethnically correct you shudda said 'yous wans', get it, man? As in 'yous wans come over here bombing pubs and living off the welfare state.' Like I mean *my* mum and dad was born over here, what about you Mr Flanagan, eh?"

Flanagan, in despair, looked round the class. Faces, white, black and brown, were closed and hostile. Groups of boys were painstakingly tearing up their remedial readers. Others were attacking the class library. The three girls, Sandra Higgs, Concepta O'Keeffe and Tiffany Finnegan, slowly removed their skirts and placed them on top of the piled-up paper. Ramesh Patel waved a box of Ship matches. Silently, desks were overturned, expert hands erected a barricade. MacKenzie leaned against his desk smiling approval, then shrugged and walked casually towards the half-naked Sandra Higgs. Flanagan, aware for the first time that cold sweat exists outside the Oxford Book of Clichés, looked round the transformed room, thought: "Jesus, what's mere about anarchy?", then picked up his books and quietly opened the door. Passing Remedial A, he heard Miss Saunders still reciting: " ... millions of seedlings under the ground/Yes millions, beginning to grow!"

He was halfway home on the bus before he woke to the fact that he ought to have called for help, rung bells, rushed off to get Briggs and the Head ...

Leaving the betting shop with an extra one pound ninety in his pocket, he picked his way through the bags of sodden rubbish that by now were spreading out in messy circles from the foot of every lamp-post (and beginning to pong a bit after seven weeks of the dustmen's strike). One or two of the women in the greengrocer's queue had copies of 'Her World' sticking up among tins of baked beans. Was this his audience? Dark roots, parched remains of perms, blackheads jutting up like dangerous reefs out of thick beige make-up. If they knew he was Jane Flanagan would they care? Or did they only buy it for their stars and the love story? Where were the carelessly elegant discontented wives he wrote about, swallowing Valium as they watched their Classics degrees being torn to pieces by chubby little fingers? They weren't buying avocado pears in Willesden Green, that was certain.

A sense of empty desolation shrank him, as it had shrunk him leaving Josie's flat that morning, and again in the staff-room, and later still in the long disbelieving seconds before he fled, shutting the door on the wreck of Remedial B. His brain refused to focus on what might be happening at the school: rape, murder, arson? The beginnings of a race riot that could spread right across

North London? His mind slid away to immediate necessities – the need to re-write his article, a few puns, a happy ending, a hundred pounds worth of sentiment to get him past rent-day. Even if nothing worse happened he'd never be offered another teaching job. He had nothing, he was nothing. And big Josie was leaving. Big Josie was real and free and young, she had no need of his pity. Big glamorous vulgar Josie bulldozing her way to adventure. And Briggs and MacKenzie, alive and real, perhaps at this very minute facing each other across the flames. So pondered Flanagan, a slight balding figure in a too-long Bogart trenchcoat, clutching a half-finished novel and two unripe avocado pears, stepping gingerly to avoid the dog-droppings of a slum pavement, a slum city. I don't exist, he whispered, I don't exist – plunging blindly across the road towards the shelter of Brondesbury Heights and his typewriter.

On the Stairs

It was the day for taking Sean to the Clinic so Mammy told her to go straight up to Miss Dolan's when she came in from school and Carmel did but Miss Dolan wasn't there and the door of her room was locked. Carmel sat on the stairs for a long time but still Miss Dolan didn't come and her mother didn't come back either. It was cold on the stairs and too dim to look at her reading-book. She heard the Ryans coming in from work laughing and talking loudly and then they banged their flat door and she was alone again in the silence. She wondered what would they say if she went down and asked them to look after her till Mammy came home from the clinic?

But Mammy didn't like the Ryans and would surely shout at her for going to their flat. The Ryans used to make much of her and bring her sweets when they came to visit and for a long time Carmel liked them and planned to marry Joe Ryan when she grew up to be a big girl of fourteen or fifteen because Sal Ryan was sure to be old and dead by that time. But then one day she drew a lovely picture for him with her felt pens and gave it to him when he came to drink beer with her father only that day he didn't even look at her, he just said yes yes, and went on talking to Daddy and he didn't even look at the picture either, not once, he just kept on folding it and folding it and talking and talking till the picture was a small fat square and then he started flicking it with his thumb-nail across the table, and catching it and flicking it again, and Carmel couldn't watch anymore and went away to sit on her bed till he left.

It was that same day that Joe Ryan and her daddy ended up shouting at each other and at first she thought it was because of him spoiling her picture but then when he'd gone Mammy started shouting too and saying the Ryans were mad in the head and if Daddy got himself mixed up in any of their nonsense she'd walk straight out and take the children with her, she wasn't going to risk getting involved in that class of carry-on no thank you and if that's what *he* wanted why didn't he go back home to the Bogside and have done with it? After that the Ryans never came back to visit and Carmel stopped wanting to marry Joe Ryan when she grew up and that's why it was better to sit on the stairs and wait for Miss Dolan.

Only Miss Dolan didn't come and the stairs were getting darker and her hands were freezing. The ceiling was very high and the stairs went on up and turned a corner into the dark where Jenny and Elaine's flat was. She could have gone up to Jenny and Elaine only they were away on their holidays. Miss Dolan never went on her holidays except for one time she went to Ireland and when she came back she told Mammy that was the very last time, she got held up and robbed by three hooligans in the very centre of Dublin and not a Guard to be seen and nobody as much as looked at what was happening to her, drug addicts and cornerboys of all descriptions, you were as well in Beirut, she said, and she was nearly always in her room reading because she finished work at three o'clock.

Love stories she read, and Mammy said that was a laugh

and the cut of her. Miss Dolan had no first name and no husband. Mammy said she was a right old maid and on the shelf for good and all. Mammy said Jenny and Elaine were on the shelf too only they hadn't the wit to realise it, running out to bars and discos at their age.

She said it to Josie in the basement and Josie laughed and said Mammy was old-fashioned and you could stay single till you were ninety these days and it was no disgrace and you could go out for a drink or a dance if you felt like it without always having to worry about hooking a man. And later Carmel heard Josie saying to Jenny and Elaine that Mammy got married late in life and wasn't too happy and it was a pity about her really, husband or no husband she must be as frustrated as hell, Josie said.

Carmel thought Jenny and Elaine were beautiful, Jenny was the nicest but Elaine was lovely too. They were always buying new dresses and when Carmel went up to their flat they let her look at their nice clothes and smell their perfumes. And one time Jenny sat her at their dressing-table and put lipstick and eyeshadow on her so that she could see what she'd be like when she grew up. Jenny said she was the image of her daddy, she was her daddy's girl, she'd grow up to be the spit of John Foley. And then they giggled a lot and said she'd have to go on a diet. Carmel was pleased because that sounded very grown-up, to go on a diet. *They* were always going on diets, Elaine said you have to suffer to be beautiful and they were ready to try anything this side of starvation. Mammy said the pair of them needed their heads examined and it was easy enough to look slim if you didn't make a pig of yourself out running to bars and restaurants every night of the week.

Miss Dolan never went to the discos or the wine bars, only up to Mass on Sunday in St Mary Magdalen's. Penny Kelly at school went to the same Mass but Mammy and Carmel took the fifty-two bus to a different Mass, to the

Carmelites up in Church Street. Mammy said there was a better class of people. Only today Miss Dolan must have gone someplace after work. She was a cashier in a hotel and went out to work very early in the morning before Carmel was awake so maybe she didn't know Mammy was taking Sean to the Clinic. Her door was just in front of Carmel's face, white and shut and empty looking, and behind Carmel's back the dark went on climbing up and up. She didn't want to look behind her at the dark.

When Jenny and Elaine were there they left the flat door open and music and light splashed down on the two landings. They had no consideration, Miss Dolan said. Jenny and Elaine were away on their holidays in a place called Benidorm. They went in a luxury coach. Daddy said they might manage to click this go-off and Mammy said what was anyone likely to click in Benidorm these days, nothing only trash went to places like that though maybe by this time Jenny and Elaine weren't too particular. Not, Mammy said, that she would ever have a chance to see what Benidorm or any other Dorm was like, her gallivanting days were over, she said, the unfortunate night ten years ago she strolled down to Biddy Mulligan's and met John Foley. And Daddy got up from the table and said if that's the way it was she could keep her flamin' dinner and shove it she knew where, he'd be in the White Hart if anyone needed him. That was last night.

Maybe Daddy didn't go to work today. He sometimes didn't go in to work after he spent the evening in the pub, he went to stand in the bookies on Walm Lane, getting rid of the rest of it, Mammy said. The rest of what? Carmel wanted to know and Mammy said Big Lugs, always hanging round when you're not wanted. If he wasn't at work he might be downstairs in the flat and he'd make a laugh of her afterwards if he knew she sat up here on the stairs in the dark. Only he might shout at her if she went down disturbing him, so in the long run it was as well to stay till Miss Dolan came and then let on she'd been in her room the whole time. Miss Dolan couldn't be long now. Maybe she went to the hospital to see poor Mr Flanagan.

Mr Flanagan got knocked down and wasn't expected to live, Mammy said. His door was nearly beside Miss Dolan's, just past the big white cupboard where the brooms and Hoover were kept. On the other side of Miss Dolan's room was a long thin passage where the Whippet's room was and beside that was the bathroom where she went to do her wet when Miss Dolan was looking after her. When you were in the bathroom you could sometimes hear the Whippet talking and laughing to himself and letting on he was beating someone, only Miss Dolan told her there was nobody there but himself. She had forgotten about the Whippet but she knew she would not see him because he didn't come in from work till half past six or seven.

Mammy would be back by then and getting her ready for bed. She imagined herself in her bright red pyjamas saying her prayers and then getting into her warm bed, jumping the last bit in case there was anyone crouching under the bed. She knew there couldn't be but she jumped anyway just in case. The Whippet would come home from work and climb the stairs and go along the passage to his room but Carmel would be downstairs by then in the bright warmth and maybe Mammy and Daddy wouldn't be fighting because when Mammy went to the Clinic she always went to have coffee afterwards with some of the other women and then she came home in a good mood.

The Whippet's real name was Mr Wordsworth but Mammy and Daddy and Josie never called him anything except the Whippet and Mammy warned her not to speak to him if he went past when she was playing out in the hall. Miss Dolan didn't call him the Whippet, she called him that awful man and she said Carmel must never let on she saw him, just walk quickly past with her eyes lowered. Carmel wanted to go to the bathroom but she was afraid to walk down the long passage. When she was with Miss Dolan, Miss Dolan went with her down the passage and stood outside the door till she was finished. Carmel wasn't really afraid of the Whippet because Josie told her he was harmless. He wouldn't touch you, Josie said, or me either, and it was scandalous, she said, to destroy an unfortunate man's character like that. He was just a lonely old man, Josie said, and his own worst enemy, so Carmel always smiled and said hello if she met him in the hall and she smiled even more on the days she wanted to spite Mammy.

But the landing was getting very dark now and so was the passage and if she wanted light she would have to stay standing with her finger on the button. She did not want to stand up. She crouched well down with the step digging into her back, the wall against her shoulder, her satchel held against her knees for comfort and she kept her eyes fixed on Miss Dolan's door. Supposing Miss Dolan was in there all the time, fast asleep? She was afraid to risk her footsteps on the carpet now, afraid of the noise her knock would make on the wood.

If Mr Flanagan died would his ghost haunt the landing? Behind her the stairs went up and up and round into the dark. She kept her eyes on Miss Dolan's door, willing her to be there, to wake up, to come out and see her. The door was very white in the dim landing, whiter than the Whippet's long face. When you said people had white faces they weren't really white. And Lorraine at school wasn't really black, just sort of greyish brown. But Lorraine said she was black and Mammy said Lorraine was black and that's why she couldn't ask her to come and play with her again in the hall. We don't want any blacks about the place, Mammy said, it's the only good thing about this dump, she said, that the landlady's particular who she takes, and don't

On the Stairs

you start inveigling them round again or I'll leave welts on you. Play with wee Kathleen in the basement, Mammy said, they're a decent class of people. Mammy was dying to make friends with Kathleen's mother because she was a teacher and a cut above the rest of them, Mammy said. Daddy said leave the woman alone what do we know about her, she could be the greatest trollop in London for all we know, handy enough these days being able to call yourself Mizz, Daddy said laughing ...

Miss Dolan didn't come and neither did Carmel's mother and the house was very quiet. She knew the Ryans were there and perhaps the other tenants downstairs and Kathleen and her mum and the landlady in the basement, but all the same she wished Miss Dolan would come. If even one person downstairs opened their door and let light out on the landing she could get up and walk downstairs ... Was it really brooms in the cupboard? It was a very big door, more like the door of a room. Supposing it was a locked room? The doors hung in the dark like sheets. Dark was like a wall that you couldn't touch. She wished the Clinic was over, but it would be better if Miss Dolan came first because then Mammy couldn't shout at her for sitting all this time on the stairs. But what else could she do? She wished there was no Clinic. She wished there was no Sean.

Once upon a time, when she was five, there was only her and Mammy and Daddy. They went to the seaside in Ireland and they went to the zoo and they went to watch Daddy kicking football in the park. She didn't remember but Mammy told her. It was before Daddy grew his beer-belly, Mammy told her. Nobody would let him near a team now, she said, unless they were paid to lose the match. Daddy was fat.

Mammy got fat too and then she got thin again. Sean grew in Mammy's stomach. She knew that was true because Josie told her. She laughed and laughed when

Josie told her because it was so funny and she asked Mammy if it was true there was a little baby growing away inside her and Mammy gave her a clatter and said such filthy dirty talk and I'm ashamed of you and you'll have to tell it when you go to make your first Confession or else our Blessed Lord will make you burn in hell. And Mammy said Josie was a bad girl with a dirty tongue and that Carmel was never to go inside the door of her flat again. Only it was true what Josie told her because Mammy had to go to the hospital and the doctor took Sean out of her stomach and she came home thin. Penny Kelly and Lorraine Jackson said *their* mummies had babies growing inside them too, and Penny said her mum let her feel the little baby kicking. Only Carmel was afraid ever to mention it to Mammy again. Mammy often hit her just for saying things or asking questions. But why did Mammy tell lies about Sean?

It would be funny if there was no Sean. First he didn't exist, he was nowhere at all, and now he existed and she would never be her Mammy's baby again or sit on her knee. She rubbed her hands together to warm them and tried to shove them up the sleeves of her coat but they were too narrow. She sat well back against the stair wall, her hands in her pockets, trying to be just another shadow in the dark in case anything was watching her. She stared straight at Miss Dolan's door, not looking to right or left of it. If she looked to right or left she might see something awful.

Poor Mr Flanagan mustn't have looked before he crossed the road, that's why he got hit. Blood everywhere, Daddy said. If he was dead he might be standing there by his own door, at the other side of the broom cupboard, looking at her. Was it true that the Whippet ate little girls? If it was true it was a terrible thing and why did Daddy laugh? She knew it wasn't true. In the daytime it wasn't true. It wasn't possible to eat people. And dragons and monsters and bombs on the telly weren't true either, they were just stories to look at. That was why she had to be a brave girl and not a dirty coward whining and whingeing when she was sent to bed on her own because Mammy was busy attending to Sean. But ghosts were true, ghosts could happen. Mammy told her. Mammy said ghosts were the poor souls in Purgatory coming back to ask for our prayers. Or if somebody was very bad and went to hell and couldn't be kept in hell then he'd have to be a ghost and wander about forever and ever. Mammy said we must be very careful about telling all our sins and being in the state of grace just in case we died suddenly or got knocked down.

Why didn't Miss Dolan come? Carmel wondered how late it was, it must be very late. It was like when you woke in the night and the whole house was asleep and dark and silent. Where was Miss Dolan? Was it possible to fall asleep without knowing and then Miss Dolan could have come back unknown to her and never think of looking on the stairs and be in bed fast asleep and it could be the middle of the night even? Carmel knew that was silly. But if Miss Dolan got knocked down crossing the street like poor Mr Flanagan?

Mammy said Mr Flanagan was carrying on something shocking with Josie in the basement. That one's no better than a tart, Mammy said, and a good thing for all of us that she's leaving, she'll be well-met where she's going, Mammy said. And Daddy laughed and said poor old Flanagan, he'd never be fit for that lassie! Daddy said in his opinion Mr Flanagan was as bad as the Whippet and Carmel asked what was wrong with the Whippet and Daddy said he ate little girls. Only why did Daddy laugh? Was it because it was only a story? And Miss Dolan said the Whippet did nasty things only she wouldn't say what.

The Whippet had a funny face with a long thin mouth, nearly no lips, and his eyes were pale. He always looked frightened. His face looked a bit like Mammy's face and Kathleen's face in the basement, pale and thin, only why would Mammy or Kathleen be frightened? People's faces didn't always look like them. *What* nasty things? When Mammy caught her tickling herself she gave her a belt across the face and said you filthy wee girl doing nasty things, I'm ashamed of you, I'll leave welts on you, she said. Mammy said God would punish her if she did nasty things or said bad talk or looked at herself doing her wet. Our Blessed Lady is looking down at you and blushing, she said. Josie said it was a disgrace to fill a child's head with such nonsense, Mammy was out of the Ark, Josie said, my God you'd never think it was the nineteen-eighties, she said, that poor kid's going to grow up with all sorts of inhibitions. But Josie was a bad girl and Josie was going away to work in France and with a bit of luck they'd get someone respectable in her place. Mammy and Miss Dolan said.

Would poor Mr Flanagan go to hell? Would he come trailing round the landing in his long raincoat with his books under his arm begging her to pray for him? Or could he be all dressed in white, with blood instead of a face? Daddy said it was a holy terror the accident. He said poor Flanagan was just after saluting him in the betting shop, he was a couple of quid up as well, and a few minutes later there was all the commotion and the squealing and Daddy rushed out and he nearly died when he saw. Blood pumping out of him, Daddy said.

Where was Miss Dolan, where was Miss Dolan? Carmel squeezed herself back against the wall staring at the dim white rectangle of door to keep herself from seeing anything else. She tried to listen for the little click of the front door but all she could hear was her own heart

On the Stairs

thumping and thumping and when she touched her chest she could feel it through her coat getting faster and faster till she thought she would choke.

Was she going to die here alone on the stairs, was God going to punish her for doing bad things? Oh my God I am heartily sorry ...

The house was dead silent. Supposing he was dead already, supposing he was there now, standing beside his own door, watching her? Was that something moving? She could hear steps, she could hear steps below in the hall, below on the stairs. Dear baby Jesus thank you for Miss Dolan, thank you for Miss Dolan! And then the steps were not Miss Dolan's steps, they were heavy steps, a man's steps. They were poor Mr Flanagan's steps, he was coming up the dark stairs all covered in blood and she wanted to scream and no voice came out and he was on the landing now coming towards her and her throat was dry and empty, no voice, and she couldn't move and she waited plastered flat against the wall waiting for him to reach her, to put his broken bleeding hand on her.

Then the landing light went on and someone was bending over her and it was only the Whippet home from work and she screamed and screamed with relief that it was only the Whippet and not poor dead Mr Flanagan with his sins pumping out of him and through her screams she heard the Whippet saying: " ... and your dad's just coming in the door and hush now, hush now child, I'll carry you down to him ... " but she couldn't stop screaming.

And then Daddy and Joe Ryan were there holding the Whippet by the shoulders and shouting: "Begod the dirty pervert, what did he do on you, what did he do? Bejasus I'll kill the bugger, what was he at?"

And she couldn't answer, she couldn't stop screaming, and she kept on screaming as her daddy carried her gently down home and Joe Ryan was kicking the Whippet and over Daddy's shoulder she could see the Whippet lying with blood on his face on the bright landing and then Joe Ryan pushed past them on the stairs, running past them on the stairs, down to the basement to ring the police, and she couldn't stop screaming.

FURNITURE

SHE'D MISCALCULATED THE DISTANCE TO ZORBA'S AND IT MADE HER feel, unaccountably, that she need expect no pardon. Don't be crazy, she thought, pardon for *what*? People go out to dinner all the time without making a whole big drama of it. But she was uneasy, began to regret the invitation, told herself she must have been mad to think the evening would be simple, let alone pleasant. Hardly turned the corner out of Brondesbury Heights and Kathleen's feet were beginning to drag, Gerry's face was a mask of tolerant impatience, and Liz had already asked, in joking irritation: "Well for heaven's sake how many more miles *is* it?"

When she arrived at Euston three weeks earlier Tessa's first impulse had been to contact her brother and, if it hadn't been five in the morning, she might well have leaped off the train and into a coin-box out of sheer habit. Waiting for the Tube to start running she killed time with a cup of station tea and reflected that ringing Gerry first thing mightn't have been a very adult gesture anyway: would she never be mature enough to deal with a crisis without wanting to go crawling for support to whatever member of the family happened to be at hand? So, in what she considered a sensible grown-up way, she booked into a reasonably cheap B&B and straight away set about the chores of ringing up the Education people to see about a job for herself and an infant school for Kathleen. It had all been far easier then she expected, though the expensive basement where they didn't mind a small child was in a dilapidated road and the school where she was to start supply-teaching had a reputation for violence. Still, as the girl in the Council office pointed out, she was very lucky to get anything with all the unemployment there was about. She was less lucky in tracing neglected friends of her student days. How could Carol and Jenny have vanished without a trace in eight years? And through what process of love and compromise had Jill turned into that plump matron in a Teddington bungalow, obsessed with her plump Christopher-Robin baby, and with so very little to say to Tessa and her pale strained daughter?

Several times loneliness almost drove her out to a coinbox to dial her brother's number and just as often pride told her to stand on her own two feet. With time to spare she rediscovered London, delighting in the forgotten freedom of being able to jump on and off buses and wander round shops without checkpoints and bomb scares. The evenings were lonely after Kathleen had gone to bed but then, she reminded herself, she'd lived through plenty of lonely evenings when she was married. When she had regrets and sudden fits of crying (only to be expected, she told herself, not being made of stone) she had just to look at Kathleen's extinguished little face, feel how the child clutched at her hand at a raised voice, a backfiring car, to know that if she'd made a mistake at all it was in putting off their escape for far too long. She was coping and would very likely continue to cope and this surprised her, because she had not been at all sure ...

When, after three weeks she could no longer resist the

Furniture

urge to ring Gerry's flat, she did so expecting applause for her ability to survive rather than pity for her plight – and was chilled when offered neither, only his cool cautious voice coming down the line with a grudging suggestion that it might perhaps be as well if they had a little family get-together to thrash things out. Taken aback by his lack of warmth and surprised he should feel there was anything to 'thrash out' at this stage, she blurted a hasty invitation to eat next evening in her favourite Greek restaurant.

So here they were, all four of them, walking down the High Road in a bus strike, through a dreary Kilburn landscape of discount shops, betting-offices and flashy furnishing stores full of chandeliers and nylon carpeting. In all her plans for the evening Zorba's had seemed just a pleasant walk away, not worth taking the Tube for and still far enough to give them a chance to chat about this and that, breaking the ice in a way that would make it hard for Gerry to play at elder brothers even if he wanted to.

Perhaps if it hadn't rained ... if they had been more relaxed to begin with ... if *they* hadn't arrived off a packed rush-hour train ... It was her own fault of course, she ought to have counted on rain, on their coming straight from work tired and hungry. What had she expected from the meeting anyhow? Gerry's attitude on the phone ought to have warned her; knowing her family how could she have imagined they would just casually accept the situation and go on from there? From the minute she opened the door she'd been conscious of their low-voiced discomfort, as though they'd caught her out in something shameful and were embarrassed by it. Now she too felt a vague embarrassment, guilt uneasily rising in her, threatening to drown her sense of all she'd achieved since leaving home.

"It can't be much further," she reassured Liz. "I didn't realise, I'm so ... I forgot about this bus thing, you see." Apologetic and, in spite of herself, pleading. They certainly weren't about to start chatting brightly about anything, heads down against the unexpected summer drizzle.

It would be better when they got to the restaurant, the lovely food, friendly waiters standing about in an imitation orange grove, the candles ... She saw, through her sister-in-law's wellbred eyes, the boarded-up offices, the large sagging women with shopping bags outside Marks and Spencers, shop windows full of plastic shoes and cheap tinselled saris. To Tessa herself, Kilburn was the colour and movement and laughter she'd missed in Casement Flats, the warm gregariousness of life before she'd moved back to Ireland with Liam. And now, mockingly: 'Back to Ireland – Fares slashed!' screeched an emerald neon sign above a travel agents. (You had the usual misty dreams of the exile – green fields and white cottages and easy friendliness. You didn't expect the built-up suburb and the council flat and a discontented husband with no job, loneliness and empty streets and the lurking threat of violence. Haggard young neighbour women whose unquiet eyes had learned to distrust new faces and strange accents ...)

"Did you hear from home?" Gerry abruptly broke the silence.

"No, not since I left."

"Mother's taking it very bad, you know, what you did. It was a hard blow for her after the way she brought us up."

"She's heartbroken, really heartbroken," Liz added.

What right has she to be heartbroken? Tessa thought, I was heartbroken, whatever it means, for long enough and little any of them cared.

"Couldn't you for once in your life have tried to settle down and put up with things like everybody else? Sure nobody expects marriage to be perfect, there always has to be some give and take."

"You should have thought of the child," Liz said. "For her sake ... "

Furniture

"It was for her sake I went as well as my own. It was insupportable, I told you in my letter, some of it, not even the worst. Why didn't you answer? I had nobody, couldn't you even have written a few lines?"

"Do try and keep your voice down, Teresa, people are looking. It's no place for a family discussion anyway, a public street, can't it wait till we get to this restaurant of yours, wherever it is?"

"Well I didn't start the discussion, you did."

"Oh God let's not squabble," Liz said, "and do we have to trek all the way to this Greek place?" Tessa wanted to laugh and be firm, say "Yes we do and to hell with the rain. I invited you out and you're going to have a good time whether you like it or not!" She no longer had the confidence to be flippant, having made them walk for fifteen minutes already.

"I mean," Liz went on in her small prim voice, "if you haven't actually booked a table we could always find a snack-bar and have a sandwich or something instead. Because otherwise ... "

Tessa could see the logic of this, dreary though it was. There was no hope now of reclaiming the evening or creating the atmosphere she'd planned. Zorba's or anywhere else, she could see herself being jostled back in time, the unreasonable young sister drumming her heels on the floor, forever in the wrong, forever screaming to be understood, in the face of their remorseless good sense.

"Mammy, where are we going to, Mammy?" Kathleen was tugging at her hand.

"For chips and ice cream, love."

"Soon?"

"Very soon."

But there didn't seem to be any snack-bars, only the endless plate-glass front of Lamerton's reflecting her chilled uneasy face in a hundred jeering mirrors.

"Well there's a place called Jilly's," she said, "there was a piece about it in *Time Out*, they do kebabs and things." Only hadn't they already passed it, wasn't it perhaps farther up, near the Villas? The rain didn't get any heavier, it slanted in thin discouragement across their cheeks and noses. They'd have been better off staying in her room, why hadn't she thought of getting in a bottle of wine and a Chinese takeaway? She looked away, into Lamerton's window. What sort of people bought furniture like that? she wondered idly to take her mind off things. She felt a stab of nostalgia for her bare-walled flat in Belfast, the whitewood furniture, her Tree of Life tapestry. She suddenly wanted to be back there enduring her life, free of decisions, free of guilt. To stop tears she peered closely at a pretentious slab of carved mahogany with matching sideboard and candelabra.

"It would appear that Jilly has strayed off into the jungles of Kilburn along with your Greek hero." (She remembered now, even when they were children she had dreaded his dry schoolmasterish sarcasm. Did his students dread it? Did his wife?)

"Look for heaven's sake, let's go in here." Liz was all sensible practicality as they approached a narrow café front with a Coca Cola sign.

"All right," Tessa agreed wearily, wanting now only to please, not to be a nuisance, though she could see the low terrace wall of Zorba's just beyond the lights, minutes away.

"How odd," Gerry said, examining a pond of tea on the pink formica table, "how odd that on the two occasions we've met in London you've managed to give me your own particular worm's-eye view of the British capital!"

She was too dispirited to point out that it was not she who had chosen this rotten café and that on their last encounter in London twelve years before, he'd been only

Furniture

too glad to accept hospitality in her student commune on his penniless way back from Majorca. (Admittedly from his point of view he'd had a right to be aggrieved: expecting the London Palladium like a good provincial schoolteacher he'd been offered instead a shared joint and an earful of Leonard Cohen. Thus had grown the legend of Tessa the family let-down, squatting amid vice and squalor in a North London slum.)

A bored waitress folded up her evening paper and trailed herself to their table with three menus and a dishcloth. Tessa buried herself behind Sausage and Chips, Fishcake and Chips, Croquette and Chips, Mixed Grill. Why was she here? What did she expect from these people, how had she ever thought they could be friends? She wanted to forget the whole thing, eat up her fishcake and leave them quickly. Get back the mood of independence and enthusiasm she'd been in before she was mad enough to phone them.

"Well I don't know what you expect of us, Teresa," Gerry said when the woman had taken their order. "Are we supposed to condone this latest folly of yours, ruining your whole life and your child's ... "

"Look I know what I'm doing, I went into it very thoroughly believe me and it seemed the only possible thing for us. You can't judge because you don't know what I was going through. You and mother, you didn't *want* to know, as long as I seemed to be living respectably and not letting you down."

"You can leave Mother out of it, you've hurt her enough after all the sacrifices she made for us."

"What sacrifices? She brought us up when Daddy died, what else could she do? She could hardly have dumped us in a Home and started running to the dances!"

"She worked hard to give us a good education and little thanks – "

"Well she wasn't exactly down on her hands and knees scrubbing floors, she was damn glad of the excuse to go back to work if you ask me. So fair enough, she sent us to the University but she might have thought of cutting our umbilical cords first."

The woman brought food in undercooked tones of beige, glancing in dull curiosity at their snarling faces. Tessa used the interruption to soothe her own anger. "Anyway I didn't ask you here to discuss it, it's over and done with and that's not why I rang you. It just seemed daft not being friends when we're both in London."

"But Elizabeth and I happen to think there's a lot to discuss." Gerry cut his croquette into small precise wedges. "I know there's no use talking to you about the sanctity of marriage because as far as I can see you never paid much heed either to your religion or your family ties, but you might at least have thought of our mother, she's not in the best of health and – "

"But it has nothing to *do* with her, can't she ever let go of us, it's my life."

"And Kathleen's." He chewed a piece of croquette. "What sort of future is it for her growing up in a poky room in a slum road. I bet you haven't even a job yet, have you? It's not so easy walking into a teaching post here you know! What do you intend to live on anyway – Social Security?" He cut up a chip and fed it into the exact centre of his mouth. Tessa watched, fascinated.

Liz turned to her: "I mean we were all so pleased that you seemed to be settling down and starting a family and we thought Liam was a very nice boy even if ... I mean I know he didn't have our advantages in life but, and then out of the blue comes this extraordinary letter criticising him and now – "

"I wasn't criticising him, he is nice, that's why I married him, but it just so happens that he's immature and violent

Furniture

and he hasn't had a job since we went back. All right I know it's not his fault but he used to take it out on me. I was at my wit's end – he used to stay out sometimes all night and I honestly never knew whether he was lying dead somewhere or lifted by the army. And I didn't know one single person in the flats, not one. Can you imagine that? In all those years! That's why I wrote to you, because I just needed to tell someone."

"Well we certainly didn't think it very loyal of you, exposing your marital problems to outsiders. And it put *us* in an awkward position, did you think of that? What did you expect us to say, how were we supposed to advise you? Everybody knows life is difficult in Belfast nowadays but there's thousands have to put up with it, they can't all run away!"

Oh what was the use, when had they ever been able to understand each other? She ate some chips, they were greasy and cool. Kathleen had picked up her fishcake and was eating it like a bun, nibbling around the edges. She'd have to try and teach her some manners. Was it the right thing for her to be here anyway, listening to the row? You never knew what was going on behind her scared eyes – perhaps she was even feeling secure because the grown-ups were quarrelling in low voices, not shouting or raising their hands to each other? There were no other customers. Outside it drizzled on. She glanced at Liz whose face expressed a vague distaste. For what – the food, the surroundings, the sordid little family scene?

"Actually I should have thought you could have joined your local church if you were as lonely as you say. If you'd really wanted to make some friends." Tessa was startled, as she had been on their few previous meetings, when faced with new evidence of Liz's totally different background. Does she think Northern Ireland's the Home Counties or what, jolly handshakes in the church porch and invite the curate home to lunch? She noted the fractional change in her brother's expression and thought for a wild moment that they might meet in shared ethnic laughter. The hope wilted – in Gerry's world you don't laugh with a sister over your wife's ignorance any more than you sympathise with her over her own husband's shortcomings. Marriage in our family's like death, she thought, they give you a great send-off, the wake and the tears and the flowers, they're sorry to lose you – only let you not come back haunting them if you don't find eternal happiness.

"The room's only temporary," she said, "while I look around. And I start work with Camden Council on Monday. I've been considering this move and putting by as much as I could, since long before I wrote to you even. I'm thirty years of age, Gerry, you don't have to worry about me. I'll manage."

She caught a small married glance between him and his wife. Could they possibly have been thinking she expected them to keep her, had they feared she'd be on their hands? Were they sordid enough to think she asked them out to get money off them? She thought not. It was involvement they were frightened of, getting mixed up in somebody else's mess.

"Well, it's something I suppose that you've made definite plans. It's more than we expected of you, I must say. But believe me it's not going to be easy bringing up a child on your own, in London of all places, you'll be sorry yet. Not to mention the moral side of it and the way you've let us all down." In a minute, Tessa thought, he'll drag Mother into it again and if he does I'll lift this plate of greasy chips and I'll –

"If I were you," Liz said reasonably, "I'd ring up your mother tomorrow and give her some reassurance. She's out of her mind with worry. Tell her you're considering things. Maybe she'd talk to Liam for you."

Furniture

Keep cool Tessa, remember you don't need these people. You can pay the bill and leave them to the Tube and never have to see either of them again ...

The rain had stopped, the High Street was a mess of street lamps swimming in wet pavements. Tessa and Liz walked together, Gerry taking his niece by the hand. No longer hungry, cold, or tired they were prepared to be nicer to one another.

"Never mind, Teresa," Liz said, taking her arm, "things will work out for you, I'm sure of it. I'll start a Novena."

Exasperated and remorseful Tessa said, to amuse her: "Would you look at that furniture!"

"I know," Liz said wistfully. "I can't wait for Gerry to finish his thesis and get a better job so that we can have a place of our own and a proper dining-room suite. *We* have our little problems too, you know!"

Surely, Tessa thought, she doesn't put living in a furnished flat on the same level as a failed marriage? Or does she think I'm eating my heart out for fake mahogany, does the bitch think that's what my style is? Or could it possibly be that Liz too was arriving at the end of some kind of tether? That smug academic wife with a flat full of Penguin classics and Solzhenitsyn on the bedside table? Behind the Evelyn Waugh Catholicism, behind Poland and Afghanistan, was there perhaps just a suburban housewife craving hopelessly for china ducks and paper doilies? The idea was so touching that she felt obliged to say: "Look it's early yet, why don't you come in and have a drink? I'll just nip across the road for a bottle of something?"

"No, no!" Gerry said quickly. "Let me get it. You come with me, Kathleen, I'll buy you sweets."

He was happy, Tessa realised, he wasn't going to be asked for anything at all, he wouldn't have to get involved. His womenfolk were suitably discussing furniture, there was to be no big scene, just the prospect of a civilised drink by the fire before he faced the last train home.

Tessa regretted having asked them back, wanted only to reach the safety of her room and lock the door on herself and her child. She knew that as long as she remained in London she would be impelled to keep on seeing them – just as tomorrow she would be unable to resist ringing Mother, to recommence the round of recriminations, self-justifying tears, and humiliating forgiveness that for as long as she could remember had been the unalterable pattern of her life.

Pieces d'Identite

SWINGING HAPPILY IN OFF THE FAUBOURG THAT EXISTED, SHE could almost believe, solely to pay homage to her body, (whole rows of shops dedicated to her beauty and well-being, passers-by whose eyes named her with delight or envy), Josie was shocked, slightly, when the doorman's smile took no account of her twenty-two years, her new slim shape, her clothes, her billowing hair. I might as well, she thought, be a pensioner needing a hand across the step ("Mind how you go, luv!"). Accustomed by now to the smiles of Paris: what's-in-it-for me smiles on Métro platforms, moist-lipped slither of a smile ("Got time for a drink, chérie?") that lay in ambush if she stopped to look in a shop window, appreciative (metaphorical slap-across-the-rump, counting-of-teeth) smile that told Christophe he knew how to pick 'em, crisp hostility of other women's' smiles busy pricing her clothes, pricing her value: accustomed after two years to all this she was for a second or two thrown off balance by the disinterested matiness of the man's grin, its simple sexless expression of a shared humanity.

"And what can I do for *you*, luv?"

"I'm getting married, I want to get married in Paris you

see, and they told me at the Préfecture they needed a copy of my ... my Police Dossier?" she finished unbelievingly.

"Thass right luv," handing her a form, "Just a formality. This lot, they get born with a wooden spoon in their mouth and a nice clean empty file with their name on all ready and waiting on Maigret's desk just in case they decide to grow up crooked."

She could tell it was a joke he'd made a hundred times but she smiled with him anyway at the unaccountable French obsession with bureaucracy. (Only, ought she to be joking with a doorman, receptionist, whatever he was: would Christophe *like* it?) She took the form with a cool thanks and turned away to fill it in at a shelf near the door.

"And what part of Ulster do you come from?"

She told him, with some hesitation. Reactions tended to be extreme. At best, shrieks of delight (Americans at a party): "But how exa-a-atic honey! Listen kids waa-o-ow! Just try and guess where this chick comes from!" At worst, pinched lips and a quick dismissive change of subject round some dinner table in a Versailles villa. (They were well-informed, her future in-laws, they read *Time* and *Newsweek* and they knew all about Catholic ghettos and shabby farming hamlets, *n'est ce pas*, and they knew exactly where she stood, socially. And it mattered.)

"A lovely place," the man said casually, "or it used to be. Ah yes, I made a lot of good friends in Ulster. Stationed over there for years I was – oh long before you were even thought of. Armagh, Londonderry, all over." He named a regiment with nostalgia, pride.

"Aw-haw the blaggards!" She snatched back the thought before it could bounce off her tongue, the phrase her father used when army helicopters swooped and dived provocatively, making cows bucklep. "Aw-haw the blaggards!" She slammed her smile shut and moved away slightly to mark a distance, regretting it instantly. Wasn't

Pièces d'Identité

this easy friendliness something she'd been homesick for off and on for ages and why throw it away for a prejudice, for a conditioned reflex? Because after all, she demanded savagely of the inconveniently insular self that lingered on, weak and undernourished, inside her composed cosmopolitan exterior, after all if you care that much why aren't you over there doing something about it? Yes, why are you here and not there? It's your place there, surely? If you're that bothered. "*I* didn't mistake Slieve Gullion for the Sierra Maestra." The sentence leaped spontaneously into her mind but, spontaneous or not, she was already wrapping it up and keeping it safe to use in a conversation sometime.

She was aware that a good bit of her time nowadays was taken up with chores that seemed minor (futile even?) but that were apparently necessary for acceptance: choosing clothes that were *exactly* right for the person Christophe's fiancée was supposed to be, reading not just any old rubbish to kill time between two stations but what everyone else was reading, building up a stock of phrases, of fresh ways to say things, small rehearsed flippancies and allusions that might go down well. She would probably change Slieve Gullion to the Mountains of Mourne: they'd all heard of the Mountains of Mourne, it meant something to them. Or would that be vulgar? (And, 'Jesus *Christ*!' jeered the awakened wisp of her nineteen-year-old self.)

She looked round for the old soldier, wanting to make up to him for her rudeness, but he was busy now attending to a boy with passport problems. She shrugged and bent to continue filling the form. O'HARE BRIGITTE she'd printed without thinking, had to cross it out and write JOSEPHINE instead. ("Josephine?" Christophe's mother asked when they were introduced. "Josie? But it's out of the Ark, chérie! My Portuguese maid's called Josephine, haven't you another name?"

"I took Brigid for Confirmation."

"But that's splendid, that's perfect darling! Brigitte, so typically Irish *n'est ce pas?*") Here, in no-man's-land, under the no-man's smile of an English doorman, she could be Josie again for a while.

"Finished, luv? Okey-doke, now you just go and wait beside the desk till they call your name out, awright?" Behind the long counter, caricaturally-English young men with soft blondish hair and nice accents were strolling around in a lanky, caricaturally-English sort of way, without fuss or gesture. She found their atmosphere gentle and reassuring, an oasis. Two French girls came in to enquire about job prospects in London; they examined Josie from head to toe with deliberate frozen curiosity. She returned their cold stare with expertise, as she'd learned to do, summing them up: their clothes were off the cover of *'Jeune et Jolie'*, their voices from the top of some suburban tower block. She gave herself a silent round of applause when they looked away first.

A slight commotion by the door and a couple of policemen, triumphant as anglers, led in an elderly battered brown-skinned man, gripping him firmly an arm each though he didn't look in the least inclined, she thought, or indeed able, to turn and run.

"Found this type wandering about Pigalle in a daze this morning. No money. No papers. *Naturellement!* British he *says.*"

They gave him a push towards the counter and he began to explain in excellent outraged English that he'd just arrived for a short holiday and got beaten up by a gang of youths in the Metro the night before. It could happen to anyone, she thought, it could happen to a bishop, he's probably a Pakistani doctor or something over to see the sights, Paree by night oh lala, and there's those rotten frog flics pushing him around as if he was an immigrant worker

Pièces d'Identité

or a tramp. (Only what the feckin hell's come over you Josie dear, mocked a silent voice in an accent she'd long disowned, what's come over ye to think it natural for immigrants to get shoved around by the law? Or tramps for that matter?")

"Not a word of French," a policeman said with virtuous disapproval, "not one single word!"

"Mais alors, qu'est ce qu'il vient foutre à Paris, le p'tit père?" one of the French girls enquired.

"He is perhaps a student from Libya?" her friend suggested, and they burst out laughing. The Pakistani stood in silent angry embarrassment.

"It's perfectly all right, you can go now," one of the clerks told the police. "We'll look after this gentlemen. D'you mind coming through here, sir?"

The French girls left, still giggling. Josie handed over her passport, birth certificate, carte de séjour, and stood idly looking round while the clerk checked them.

A woman burst bright as a butterfly through the door, shook hands with the doorman, and waddled on short fat legs towards the desk. Royal blue dungarees and eyeshadow and a plastic comb in her lacquered blonde curls. Too blonde, too lacquered, but the face beneath was one Josie had encountered a thousand times in London, plump with ignorant good nature. Face above a loaded trolley: "Tea's oop, lassies!" Face behind a canteen hatch, dishing out Labour Exchange scandal along with the stuffed marrow and gravy, face that took your fares in the fifty-two: "Full up inside luv, seats on top, move along there move along, plenty of seats up top!"

Nostalgia made Josie beam a welcome and move over to make place at the desk. (Nostalgia, but who'd want to go back all the same?)

"Do excuse me, won't you dear," the woman said, "but I want to catch this young man before he goes off to his lunch." She addressed the clerk: "Was there ... I mean did you remember to *ask*, dear?" "I'm sorry, really frightfully sorry, but there wasn't a thing, they want qualified people you see, that's the problem, you're not trained. You haven't the qualifications, that's what they said."

Josie guessed at the embarrassment behind his sympathetic courtesy, guessed he was clinging to the word 'qualifications' like a straw: what he meant and couldn't say was 'youth', 'presence', 'decent clothes'. She was glad, for the woman's sake, that the two French girls had left.

"But I've dozens of references dear, did you tell them? I always worked for Embassy families, always. Before my marriage of course. Thought the world of me. Nanny Glad they used to call me, that's my name, Gladys. Even send me cards still at Christmas, some of them. Of course they're all scattered ... Did you tell them I'd be willing to do housework, dear? Not the rough of course, but Nanny Glad was never one to be scared of a bitta dusting, not 'er!"

"It didn't make any difference," he said sadly, "they all have Portuguese and Filipinos for that, you see." "Look," he continued earnestly, "I'll ask again, all the young couples I know, I'll ask around for you. There may well be something."

"How kind, how very kind you are," she murmured in amazement, as though kindness had become something very scarce and very precious.

She turned to Josie: "It's hard to make ends meet nowadays, don't you think? I've my widow's pension of course but it doesn't seem to go as far as it used. Thirty-two years I've been here dear, stayed on when my poor 'usband passed away. It's a glorious city don't you find? You'll love it here, dear, the parks, the museums, the river. So nice and clean for a city I always think."

For something to say Josie mentioned that she was going to an exhibition at the Louvre after lunch.

"Might run into each other then, I often pop down of an afternoon meself. You a student dear? There's nowhere like Paris, is there? Couldn't live anywhere else, I couldn't. Well I suppose I'd look a bit daft going back to live in Maidstone now. I don't know one single living soul in Maidstone, would you believe it dear?"

She was lonely, garrulously boring as the lonely are, and longing to talk. Josie would have liked to stay and chat, ask her to have a coffee somewhere. (Because imagine no longer knowing a single person in your home town!) But she couldn't stay, she had to meet Christophe and another couple for lunch. She said it would be nice if they did run into each other in the Louvre and, shaking hands, made up her mind to ask Christophe's mother if she knew of a suitable family. She could always leave a message at the Consulate ...

Rushing back down the Faubourg (silk scarves and Gucci shoes), being swallowed by a Métro, spat out again on the Rue de Rivoli (gilt lighters and Penguin books), hurrying to find the café, she agreed that it *was* lovely, that it was glorious, that even if one had no money, no job, no friends, it must still be worth it to live amongst such beauty, so close to the heart of life.

She sipped her apéritif on a terrace full of well-dressed people: young, attractive, united by grace and intelligence. Crisp-edged Spring sun teased her face, breeze lifted her hair, Christophe was adorable and his friends full of charm. The pretty chiming in her ears, she thought absently, must come on the wind from the bird-sellers on the Quai. Only on second thoughts, wouldn't it be too far to hear, and since when did birds sing Mozart?

"It *is* Mozart?" she asked, and Christophe smiled: when they met six months ago she wouldn't even have noticed the chimes. He was pleased with her progress.

"Yes, the church over there, the bells ring a carillon at

noon. We can go and visit it if you like after lunch."

All over Paris clocks would be striking twelve, calling friends to meet friends, lovers lovers, to eat, drink, look at pictures and churches.

"All the clocks in the city," she told them, "began to whirr and chime."

"What ... ?"

"W H Auden. I've forgotten the next bit."

"Aah."

Auden doesn't matter, is minor, Auden has nothing to tell us: that's what their polite monosyllable was saying. What came after that line? Or before it? Miss Trainor at school used to play them the record, Dylan Thomas reading it. Such a long time ago, the Convent and Taffy Trainor who wasn't Welsh but had an old maid's crush on a dead poet. Five years, she thought, she'd been an adult now for half a decade. Belfast, London, Paris: she'd lived in three cities in three different countries. The terrors of her childhood were finished, the nightmare of her teens. Or nearly finished, because even now – here in shelter, loved, protected, safe across two seas – she could still remember getting off the school bus, and the long trembling walk home on dark evenings when anything could happen.

The others were discussing a new film. Words drifted through a mist of Auden, Pernod, Mozart: "Masterpiece ... Chef d'oeuvre ... nightmare and reality ... symbolic value ... " Whirr and chime, what came after whirr and chime? The girl at the next table had a lovely skirt, Josie wondered where she got it. The girl caught her looking and returned her stare, examining with insolent envy her angora jersey.

"Yes yes I see what Rosi's doing but one can't possibly ... mais non, mais non! Garcia Marquez doesn't write on that level ... Deuxième degré ... but yes I tell you ... recurring of the motif ... even way back with Macondo surely Macondo couldn't exist on any simple level, quite apart from ... surely Macondo's nothing more than one gigantic symbol, don't you agree, Brigitte?"

Josie jerked to attention; the Mozart was finished, the waiter bringing another drink. She hadn't seen the film but Christophe had made her a present of all those weird books, telling her it was essential to have read them. She *had* read most of them. Vaguely. The one the film was about she couldn't place at all, must be one of the boring ones with no dialogue that she meant to go back and read later. But Macondo ... wasn't that a marketplace with hot sunshine and a dentist pulling the mayor's teeth? She wished they wouldn't go on so much about symbols, she was hopeless at symbols. And how could she say anything intelligent about a film she hadn't bothered to see, a book she'd never got round to finishing?

She felt a moment's panic as though they were sitting there testing her, as though her whole relationship with these people was a series of roadblocks to be got through, as though her whole future depended on what she said. Macondo, a wide market square where queer brutal things happened. The Equator, intense heat, boredom. Bleak grey houses where dreams died behind the mean-eyed windows ... No, she remembered, in Macondo it was birds that died, committed suicide, smashed themselves against the shutters. Was that a symbol? Could she mention it? The banana-workers on strike and the soldiers endlessly patrolling. Helicopters like fat droning flies. And bullets cracking off an altar, and the bus where homegoing workers stepped off into gunfire? Only surely that wasn't in the book. Or was it? Or was it not another town altogether? A town with a sentry on its shoulder and an iron-clad monster growling at its back (flies rising from its belly to buzz and pry around the lost innocence of a landscape).

What symbolism would they see in her childhood memory of a green railed lawn where murdered village constables played croquet with revolvers ready at their hips? In the violation of blackberried fields, rape of a schoolgoing road? What symbolism in banana-pickers machine-gunned in Macondo? Homesick and tense and wanting to assert herself she blurted: "Well honestly I can't see that it's just a symbol, I mean it must be nightmare enough living in a place like that, I mean it's all very well for us sitting here in shelter drinking apéritifs, I mean ... " She trailed off conscious of silence, of her own idiocy. Christophe's face, as she expected, frowning. The wrong answer, his face was saying, the raw answer, you can take Brigid from the bog ... But big Josie's great hairy hooves will always be stuck halfway up a mountain, she thought foolishly.

She turned away in shame and noticed, crossing the street, a pair of bright blue dungarees screeching like a blasphemy through the harmony of jeans, silk shirts, lamb's-wool sweaters (discreet colours of earth and sand and sea, symbol she wondered doubtfully of what well-bred refusal to ever stand up and let life hit you a slap across the jaw?). Other tables were looking too as the woman reached the pavement, face serenely full of her delight in the picturesqueness of a narrow side-street, café terrace, proximity of the Louvre, a memory of Mozart ringing noon. There was a rustle of giggles, a movement of youth closing ranks as the woman went to a table alone and ordered coffee and croissants (her *lunch*?).

The girl with the pretty skirt threw Josie a smile of complicity, including her against the outsider. She was ashamed at feeling so flattered. Whispers winged from table to table: "Would you look at the dungarees! Mais regarde-moi comme elle est fringuée ... " "Thinks she's twenty." "She's cracked of course." "Cinglée!" "Has to be English in a get-up like that! Oh sorry Brigitte, I didn't mean to ... " There was an embarrassed silence at the table. She said into it, clearly: "But why apologise, Marc? I'm *not* English." Christophe's frown again. Forget it, he was saying, don't make an issue of it. Be discreet, his face was telling her, why keep shoving your foreignness in our faces? (If I marry him, if I stay here, I'll have to spend my life sandpapering the rough edges, chopping off the bits that stick out. They don't like bits sticking out, they can't cope with the unexpected.)

The waiter put coffee and croissants on the woman's table; she thanked him with a smile he didn't bother returning. Thirty-two years ago the woman must have been Josie's age, blonde and pretty and enthusiastic, sipping Pernod at a café table on her day off from nannying some diplomat's brats. Full of delight in a beautiful new city, her friends, a new and extraordinary life, all the clocks in the city chiming her a welcome. Or a warning.

Josie saw herself in years to come (widowed, abandoned, crippled or half-blind) trailing a disgraceful body through this cold and lovely city dedicated to youth and beauty and talent. (I could go, I could get up and go back on the next plane to Brondesbury Heights and the things I can cope with. There's nothing settled yet. I'm not really committed. I could still go back.)

But the people at the next table flicked approving eyes over her with casual acceptance, Christophe smiled forgiveness, and Brigitte knew she would not go back.

She scraped her chair sideways, let hair fall across her face, in case the ridiculous old English woman should see her, shame her with a smile or a wave. Compromise her forever with an acknowledgement that, for a few minutes, they'd trodden the same earth.

Escape

MEMORY IS THE SMELL OF NOVEMBER, DAMP COATS JOSTLING ME out of the Tube to a suddenness of floating treetops and the park railings rubbed out by mist. It's hurrying down Queensway past singing boutiques and the scents of foreign grocers and the street musician's banjo dropping flurries of thin notes like a scatter of loose change. Memory's the coloured push of crowds surging home from work. Student cafés, nests of steam and green trailing plants and world-defying argument and Dylan on a long-ago jukebox. It's a cherry tree in blossom on the corner of Ulsterville Avenue after a party, in a far-off peacetime dawn. The shady glitter of Rembrandtsplien at midnight, squatters along the Amstel and Neil Young wailing from every houseboat. It's blondness of desert, ripe oranges on trees, laughing guitars on the beach at Eilat. It's people above all, groups of people dotted down the highways of my past – talking, singing, fighting, lovemaking, laughing. Memory is never a solitary figure in a landscape. Now is.

Now is me in a tall grey house alone, most of the time, with the children. And with books and records and newspapers and flowers, and friends who come for summer weekends saying: "God but you're lucky, everyone should live like this!" For two days we talk of the world situation, of pictures and plays, of famine and the arms race, of good wine and food, of Ulster and Ethiopia, Chile and the Lebanon. Then on Sunday evening the others take train, plane, or car for their return trip to reality, leaving us once again alone among the fields and the flowers. For a while after they've gone my life seems not so much the pot of dreams at the end of the rainbow – more a saucepanful of domesticated dreams simmering away to itself. Battery dreams, oven-ready. I am a housewife, mother of two.

Down there in the village, some kilometres away, is another reality. Young women with small children and homes full of laughter, wedding groups on the sideboard and friends in for coffee. Chat and giggles and recipes for jam, talk of football and crops and the council elections and who died or was born. I would like them to call on me sometimes, the smart young village mums in their vivid nylon aprons. I would like to go to their houses, be (only sometimes) one of them. Try on each other's clothes, giggle and gossip. "What could you possibly *say* to them?" Adam sneers. "What have you in common?"

"Humanity?" I suggest.

"Pretentious bitch!" he retorts.

My house is surrounded by other people's fields. I have no control over the ploughing, sowing, spreading of manure, or over the combine harvesters that sway with awkward grace across my front yard, scattering children and hens. My life is bounded by the silent watchful women from neighbouring farms who, from time to time, work all day outside my windows. While they are there I dare not read a book, listen to a record, sit on the floor with endless cups of coffee, play hide-and-seek with the baby among the bedclothes. My tall windows (such a lovely view of the countryside) give the countryside a lovely view of me. Glancing in (and how often they do glance!) they expect to see, as in other houses, a competent woman going about her traditional duties. I have a role to play and cravenly I play it: carry piles of linen from ironing-board to cupboard, meticulously sweep out corners, dust on top of tall presses, speak sharply to my daughter, check the casserole on the stove, using wide unambiguous gestures as if on a stage or altar. I wonder occasionally if I am not being slightly neurotic in my desire to appease them? But how do otherwise: I am the prisoner of their inquisitive ferret faces and razor-blade eyes.

Often though, while they are there, I throw an alibi (shopping-bag) into the boot of the car and drive off to Cap Frehel to sit on the cliff's edge for hours listening to a thousand seabirds screech nonsense to themselves and each other. They are as disorganised and noisy and gregarious as I used to be: leaping suddenly into the air, making mad dives to grab an impromptu bite to eat, throwing themselves on a rock without reason for a cuddle or a gossip, jostling one another off the edge, forming endless illogical contacts. I miss contacts, am occasionally weary of solitude without anonymity. Today I can't go to Cap Frehel. I can't go anywhere to escape the relentless silent busy-ness of the countryside. My husband has gone to Paris and has taken the car. The women are working close to my kitchen windows. I am a goldfish taking care to move fins and tail in the accepted fashion. I prepare lunch for Kate and me, a bottle for the baby. The postman drives into the yard. Dear Eve you *are* lucky to be out of the rat-race, redundancy rears its ugly head. Dear Eve, our branch in Belfast got bombed again. Dear Eve write soon, tell me more about France – you can't think how refreshing it sounds, forty floors up, in a New York Fall.

The women have been joined by their husbands, arriving on tractors from far-off fields, and they're lunching in the only patch of shade, under my walnut tree. I smile bonjour, they smile bonjour, Kate come along say bonjour to the people, where's your manners? (She has plenty of manners but I overreact, fearing she'll be found lacking.)

I could sit down now and answer my three letters while they're still fresh but I'm embarrassed to sit down in front of them. There's a million things to be done in a house if you put your mind to it. So they say. I could write upstairs but supposing they thought I was having a lie-down? I want to be accepted, can't bear to be thought foreign and through-other. What I can do is take Damian for a walk in the pram: conscientious mère de famille, that is acceptable surely even in the middle of a working day? For once I will go to the village, meet other women with their babies, force myself on them with a smile, talk nappies and strained dinners walking four abreast between the hedgerows eating blackberries, be part of their cosiness. I have passed them sometimes in the car with their vivid prams and their toddlers and their shrieking happiness; I cannot forever stay aloof. I pack orange juice and rusks in my shoulder bag, quickly wipe Kate's face. She is excited, so am I. An afternoon without solitude, without books and the World Service and middle-class culture, an escape to the small realities. As a rule life satisfies me but sometimes I need to mitch. The farm women are only a pretext.

I very seldom take the left-hand path that leads to the village, preferring usually to walk in the other direction towards lake and woods. The lane is bright with haws and rosehips, dark with sloe, elder and late blackberries. Leaves are yellowing, fern turning to bracken. I plan to collect great armfuls on the way home to stand in stone jars around my rooms. But will the women see me as a foreign witch pulling weeds out of the hedges? (Here in exile I find I am chronically tethered to childhood anxieties – our family's nickname was Terrier, The Terrier Tinleys, and one Saturday coming from Confession, dolled-up Convent teenager gathering primroses, I was leaped on and thrashed by a crowd of tormentors from the Council houses.

"Hie boys wud yez look at the wee Tinley one with her prayer-book. She must be lookin for rats in the ditch!"

"Why are you laughing, Mummy?"

"Oh because it doesn't matter at all!" And it's true – I've been free for a long time now. Free of the spite and the jeers, of the narrow intolerant streets and the grey council walls. Unreasonably I sigh for that tree of withered cherry blossom as I stir a casserole sweet with alien herbs.

Madame Briand lives at the far end of the lane in a new cream-coloured bungalow with wrought-iron decorations and rustic seats on the lawn. We met and exchanged smiles in the village shop months ago, both very pregnant. Standing at her gate now, as I manoeuvre pram and daughter past cowclap and tractor rut, she calls: "Come in and see the baby!" So it will not be difficult; I have already made a contact. Sons are compared, four months old both of them, we mention weights and feeds and brands of milk. ("He's a lovely child." "Yours too." "A fine boy." "Lovely blue eyes.")

"Will you take something, Madame? Though I'm afraid I haven't any tea. Do you ever drink cider?" "Oh yes I'd love some cider, I'm becoming quite Breton haha!"

She dusts a chair and sits me down at her kitchen table. Shyly I look around. There are imitation beams painted in Light Oak Gloss, something I haven't seen for years. (Daddy long ago painted our kitchen, Dark Oak for the ceiling, Light for the chairs and, for evenings afterwards, head buried in arms, crouched on my knees, I welcomed like an addiction the oily brown smell that rasped through my nose and throat as I dreamed, joyfully, sorrowfully, gloriously, through decades and mysteries.)

The warm little memory makes me tolerant of kitchen

units in artificial teak, outsize fridge, wall mixer, cocktail cabinet, colour telly topped with plastic tulips in a plastic pot, Disney playpen and electric grandfather clock lined up to cover every inch of the room's perimeter. My husband and friends would be condescending: "The procession of gadgets, the mail-order consumerism!" How often I've heard them at it. Heard myself. Full of goodwill I think: how nice! How nice and unpretentious and warm it is, a nest of a room made for a good chinwag over steaming teacups. (And wonder guiltily if my approval is itself condescending.) She pours out two thick pottery bowls of cider. I say: "I'm *so* glad I came this way, I was wondering if – "

A pretty three-year-old girl rushes in from the garden and, ignoring us, searches intently for something in her toy-chest.

"Come here instantly Carine, where's your manners, come and kiss the lady!" Carine glances up briefly and continues her search. "Come here immediately, can't you see there's company, come and kiss the visitor when you're told!"

"Non. Non, j'veux pas!"

The mother's voice rises to a shriek: "Come and kiss Madame at once or I'll take the stick to you!"

Carine runs out, her mother after her. I sit embarrassed, Kate cringes away in case I order her to kiss the strange woman. The child returns, sobbing.

"*Now* will you kiss Madame or do I have to give you the same over again?"

Tactfully I bend to her level and she leaves a slime of tears and snot across both my cheeks. I sip my drink.

"I'm afraid my daughter's not used to social kissing," I apologise. "We don't go in for it much in my country." ('In my country.' I listen to myself sounding like every caricature of an immigrant. I take a large slug of cider and stealthily wipe the stickiness off my face.)

"You have a lovely house," I say, "and so handy for the shops."

"Yes it's – Carine Carine leave that baby alone at once. Take your filthy hands off its face or I'll take the stick to you again."

"Oh he doesn't mind, he's very sociable, loves being messed about."

"All the same she has to learn, she can't expect to be let do what she wants. Go out and play Carine, play with the little girl."

When she speaks to her daughter her voice is a high monotonous screech; she lowers it to address me: "I often thought of popping down to see you but I didn't like ... they say the English prefer to keep to themselves."

"I'm not English actually, I'm Irish."

"But it's all the same isn't it, the same country?"

"*We* don't think so," I laugh, "there's a world – "

"Carine Carine let the little girl play with your doll, don't be so selfish. She has a filthy character that child. God knows I punish her enough but it makes no difference, she can't be got to share anything. Is yours like that?"

"Oh at that age you can't really expect – "

She darts across the room, snatches the doll, and hurls it on top of the fridge.

"Now get out, get out and play in the sand you selfish little bitch, you shame me in front of the people. Get out now and give my head peace." She pushes Carine out of the room. Kate, bewildered, follows. The kitchen no longer seems cosy and intimate. I want to go home but it's too soon for politeness.

"What was I saying Madame? Yes, I often think of you down there in that old barrack of a place with no one to talk to. You must find the time long."

"Well I don't really," I say. "There's the children and

then I can usually find something to occupy me."

"Yes there's always something to do in a house isn't there? Still it's not good for you is it, spending all your time on housework, gets you down doesn't it, gets you depressed. Well I know it gets *me* down and I'm not nearly as badly off as you, they say you haven't even the telly or anything, couldn't you coax your husband to get one? It' take you out of yourself, be a bit of company like."

"Oh well," I begin.

But she's rushing on: "Mind you I couldn't live in an old house like that, I wouldn't stand for it, I'm used to having everything nice, I am. It's only rented isn't it, your house? I expect you'll be looking for something better, I mean even if you didn't want to build, well it's not easy for everyone to build, is it nowadays? But you could easily find a nice modern bungalow to rent, you know. I'm surprised your husband doesn't – "

"But we – "

"They were just saying in the baker's yesterday, it's no life they were saying for a young woman like you, a foreigner and everything, stuck out in the middle of the fields like that, no decent furniture or anything they were saying. You want to stick up for yourself, Madame, they don't realise, men just don't realise what we – "

I have a brief angry vision of the village harpies, heads together like hens under a bush, discussing me with avid ignorant pity. I swallow down half the cider at once to stop myself snarling at her. "I, uh, was thinking we might take the children for a walk," I suggest.

"A *walk*? Oh d'you think? Where is there to go though? There's nowhere to walk is there?"

"There's the lanes," I say, surprised, "or the road even. I've often seen women pushing prams out on the road."

"Common, I know who you mean, they're dead common those ones, just go to wave at the lorry drivers and chat up workers on the building-sites. You'll get yourself a bad name if you go walking with that lot, you've got to be careful, Madame, in a place this size. Once you're catalogued that's it."

"All right," I say patiently. "We could go down past the chapel, there's all sorts of lovely shady places to walk them. Don't you ever walk your baby?"

"It's the getting ready," she sighs, "getting dressed and made-up and getting them dressed. You don't know what that Carine one's like, it's too much trouble really. And then the way they gossip here, they'd say it'd fit me better to stay in and tidy the house. *No*body goes out walking just like that, Madame, not on a weekday."

"The house is lovely," I say firmly, "and you *are* dressed. You don't need make-up to go for a walk." I listen to myself with dislike (social worker? village schoolmarm?) and rush on: "Just dump the baby in his pram and we'll take the girls by the hand. We can have a nice chat. And look, I brought along a plastic bag for blackberries, it's hanging with them round there, big juicy ones."

"Blackberries? Whatever for?"

"Well, to make jam; don't you make blackberry jam then?"

"Oh thanks for the compliment, I'm not a gypsy you know, to go gathering fruit round the roads. I can afford to buy all the jam I want." She sounds deeply offended and I, blushing with guilt, wonder what buried sensitivity I can possibly have touched. To what childhood anxiety is *she* inescapably tethered?

Trying to mend matters I rush on foolishly: "Oh but it's great fun. When I was a child in Ireland – "

She puts my Irish childhood to flight with a sudden screech: "Carine! What are you doing? I can't see you, what are you up to? Oh God that brat, I haven't a minute's peace, she's trying to bury your daughter in the sand, look!"

Kate is buried up to the knees and seems to be enjoying it.

"What does it matter? All kids do that."

"But her good sandals, and her socks. They'll be ruined, they'll be filthy!"

"It's no harm, I can rinse them out can't I? Let's go in and finish our drinks. It's not really important is it?"

"I have no rest with that child," she wails, grabbing her out of the sand, washing her hands under the tap. "All day long I'm after her and it doesn't do one bit of good. I'm worn out at the end of the day shouting and beating her and she's just as bad after. It's no life, Madame, that's what I say and then he comes home expecting to be waited on hand and foot, his dinner on the table, the house clean, and all he wants is his own satisfaction, he doesn't care what I go through all day. It's no life, is it Madame, stuck in a house all day with two small children? They never think of that, do they?"

"Oh it's not too bad," I begin weakly, "I quite enjoy – "

"Carine Carine what are you up to now? Come here and tell me what you're doing! Oh God what I have to put up with, you wouldn't believe it, and I'm not right in myself at all not since the baby, not well at all, the doctor had to give me tablets. Had you a bad time with yours? What I went through Madame, wait till I tell you ... "

Dismayed, I realise that she's describing her confinement and inviting me to describe mine. I try not to hear the details of contractions and blood transfusions and milk yield and concentrate on remembering a line from Sartre, from what's-this-book, something about the average Frenchwoman, *'quand elle ne parle pas de son interieur elle parle de ses interieures,'* wasn't that how it went? I must remember to look it up when I get home. If I ever get home – I feel that I'm a prisoner in this nasty little kitchen, at the mercy of this poor miserable hag of a woman ready to discuss her tripes with every stranger who passes along the road. I desperately want to be at home with my books and my dreams, telling stories to my daughter, running to see what my husband's brought me from Paris. I drink the rest of my cider and make noncommittal replies. It is not very good cider. I realise that I'm thirty-four years old and happy and privileged, and decide that maybe it's time I started to make something positive out of my life. Only what? What's there to do? Create a wildflower garden? Have more children? Write? I used to want to write years ago ... Then I look at the empty cider bowl and wonder if it was not too large and too full. "Actually I think it's time I was going."

"No, stay a bit Madame, stay till I warm up some coffee! It's great to have someone to confide in isn't it, we don't often get the chance either of us, do we? You're in no hurry are you Madame? I'll put the telly on later, give you a bit of a change."

"No, really I must go, the baby's feed and everything. I'll come earlier another time and we can go for that walk."

She leaves me to the gate, words still splashing out of her like tears and, inadequately I say goodbye and make vague plans for another meeting.

Once turned the corner Kate begins to laugh at nothing and I join her. We gather armfuls of bracken and coloured leaves, linger to watch the changing sky. Already in my head I'm busy editing the visit into an entertaining self-mocking anecdote for my husband and I hate myself for my snobbery. I'm aware that in any case it is dishonest to cast her as the typical French housewife, obsessed with her housework and her insides, just to nourish my self-defensive racism (Eve, minority group of one). She's not a typical anything. You could meet her anywhere, in Dublin or Belfast, Epsom, Ealing or Chicago – one of those poor dispirited women sitting in a houseful of gadgets, swallowing Valium to keep going. Once I would have tried to help, that's the worst of it, once I would have been prepared to spend dreary hours listening to her griefs. Now, insulated by my own happiness, I see no need to play at Good Samaritans. Warm in the shelter of marriage I'm no longer inclined to go gustering through the muck and dirt of other people's miseries.

A pale moon is suddenly, precociously, there in the white sky. Our house stands tall and grey among fields and flowers. The women are still there, humping creels of cider apples on to trailers. The baby is asleep. I put him to bed, pour cold drinks for Kate and me, put on a record to remove the taste of the afternoon. We sit on the doorstep and Daniel Viglietti fills the bare whitewashed kitchen behind us. *Blanca corria la luna* – violin and guitar and a child lying awake in a shanty town at the other end of the world watching the moon race past the holes in a tin roof. An old record from my student days and I remember when it made me cry with its beauty and its relentless understatement of human misery. It doesn't make me cry now. It has no connection at all with the life I now lead in my cool grey house among the flowers. As I listen the shanty town comes alive with poor boring Mrs Briands screeching at their children and going noisily demented with their own discontent. Human suffering is not a bit beautiful and on the whole I'd rather not be involved.

The sky gets dimmer, the moon higher and brighter. A small plane creeps home, like a late bee, to Dinan aerodrome. High above it a jet flies westward to London, Shannon, New York. Out there, somewhere beyond those fields, is the world and reality. Sobbing of the unloved, screams of the tortured, slow grey nightmare of the hungry. And out there, (already born?), the one whose insane finger on the button will make nonsense of our dreams and our discontents, our hates and anxieties, the shelter or the prison of our marriages. There's nothing I can do about it, nothing I want to do about any of it, only sit on the doorstep with my child, watching the moon, and selfishly hug to myself the treasure of these few quiet contented years. *Ah luna, mi luna blanca*!

I am not a monster. I am Eve, a loving mother, a nice intelligent person. Everyone says so. No need for guilt – nice people are like me, for the most part. So why do I feel as though I'd taken a test and failed it? And why does Memory sneer?

The women go home in groups across my front yard.

"Lovely evening, Madame."

"Yes, isn't it? Lovely."

A Novel about the Famine

As poor as a spider? He closed the book and looked with a stranger's eyes down the meadow, attempting to impose some more desolate past on the boggy fields. But ... Poor as a *spider*? The countryside dead of hunger, as poor as a spider?

His mother took him out a cup of tea, enquired what progress he was making, said your poor granda lord a mercy on him would have been the man to instruct you, your granda was a terror once you got him started on the old times. She herself knew nothing beyond the customary emotive words: landlords, coffin ships, Black and Tans, priests hunted down like wolves, Connolly shot in a wheelchair – superimposed and interwoven to form a pious collage of eight centuries' martyrdom. His father spoke of being young in the hungry Thirties, hired out to hard-jawed Protestant farmers up beyond the Black Banks, crossing over to Scotland to pick praitas; hinted at an ancestor, a famous jockey, who made a runaway marriage with one of the Reed family, big landlords over in the County of Monaghan, now *that* would have been the time of the famine near enough.

Owen thought it might be worth following up but his

father could think of no one to consult, the Reeds died out generations ago. Jack Maguire was the jockey's name but sure the country was full of Maguires. Owen laughed: "Probably all descendants. Just call me Owen of the Maguirevilles!" But, behind the flippancy, reflected that it might be worthwhile looking up the Reed family in Dublin Castle library or someplace; he'd have to take a run up to Dublin anyhow one of these days.

Meanwhile he drank his tea which was too strong and too sweet, looking round the ornamental patio garden his father was constructing on the site of the old street: a forsythia bush, azaleas in tubs, Queen Elizabeth roses. The outhouses were gone. In his childhood the street had been surrounded on three sides by zinc-roof buildings: dwellinghouse, barn, byre for two cows, pighouse, dairy. On the fourth side had been the dunghill with its shifting cloud of blue flies. The street had been bisected by a straight line of flat raised stones. He supposed that had a significance too. A century ago, when the outhouses were still a cluster of dwellings (Maguiresville? Claghan MacEighire?), the stones would have marked out a boundary between neighbours; he wondered if they were still there beneath the concrete.

When he was six years old he stood on one of the stones in a dream, spread his arms and took off, flying gently around the street at a height of two feet, round and round and round, quietly delighted with himself. As he drifted past the byre he reached out and touched it softly with his hand, watched it crumble silently away. He drifted on touching in turn the barn, pighouse, dairy, the whitewashed walls of his home, touching currant-bushes and sycamore trees, watching in terror and delight as they crumbled to nothing and he was alone drifting endlessly over the endless fields; crying because he was alone but intensely happy because the fields were endless, and his.

But the fields had been endless even when he was

A Novel about the Famine

awake. This shrunken meadow below the terrace (shrunken to near nothing: a few steps would take you down to the kesh now) he remembered as a plain of battle, pampas of adventure, wild savannah of a child's imagining. Slow dark hedges still crawled up Paddy's field, Jemmy's field, past Murphy's rock up to Maginn's haggard. Hawthorn and wild rose, blackberry and boortree, a langelled goat that, no but those hedges, how old would they be, he wondered, would they even have been planted the time of the?

And who is there to ask, now that Paddy's dead and Jemmy's dead, and Jamesy Murphy and Maginn are dead, and your grandfather's dead? Men who were a link, whose own fathers (not forefathers mind you, *fathers*) one awful day hoked and scrabbed with wildfaced intuition at withered September drills, slowly drew out hands slabbered with corruption, examined them vaguely, smelt them vaguely, wiped them vaguely on the back of that ditch, on those weeds there, muttered a curse or muttered nothing, then paced with bent shoulders down across that kesh and home. Possibly not yet totally aware of the implications.

Home would have been the one-roomed windowless stone house hunkered down under the two big sycamore trees, here on the very spot where he was sitting. The place where his father used to keep pigs to fatten, oh it must have been thirty years ago. A zinc roof that the branches scringed along on winter nights but it would have been thatched in the time of. The time with which, he realised now, there remained no link at all.

("No," he told Joanna over the phone, "no I'm not having much luck I'm afraid; it seems the old men are all dead." She laughed, injuring him: "They were dead already ten years ago when we were over there on our honeymoon, wake up, Owen! It's just a backward little place you should have grown out of by – " He put the phone down sharply on the end of her sentence.)

His father used to keep two pigs but in that time the house would have lodged whole families, thirteen or fourteen children kicking a blown-up pig's bladder through the dust of the street, slapping barefoot down narrow pads between bogholes, dark bog-mud squeezing warm (he remembered how bog-mud was warm, even in winter) up between their bony toes.

Would they have been the well-grown beautiful children of noble mien described in the sentimental history books of his schooldays, or had they been as stunted as peasants everywhere at the time, short-legged and rickety with vacant skull-faces? There was no-one to tell him now, all the old men having slipped away in the empty years he was drifting vacantly around the world, not even consciously thinking about this place. Oh there were little references in books yes, clergymen's letters home to England: "Can you do anything for my wretched people?" And a schoolmistress who wrote articles on local history for the *Irish News* lent him photos but those turned out to be of a later date, a more prosperous date, plump shawled women (such as still existed in his childhood) selling chickens on Claghan square on a fair day. "We'll all be dead and gone," this history teacher said contemptuously, "we'll all be in our graves before this book gets written." Fed, he supposed, by some village rumour of his exploits, non-exploits, she had already cast him as a failure and he instantly saw himself through her eyes, a slight hesitant man with an apologetic face looking up at her as she stood her ground there, plump and brisk and middle-aged in a good grey suit, in his parents' new bungalow. She was a publican's daughter: well-thought-of family, noted collectors of Dues, lifters of gate-money, handers-round of collection plates. She'd been a county camogie player in her time, a Gaelic speaker, great bullier long ago of puny small boys on the way home from school. But kind, it was kind of her to bother, he told himself; she needn't have, after all, feeling as she apparently did.

What happened was, he rang her up and said: "I'm writing about the Great Famine; would you help me at all?" and she immediately loaded up her car with old documents and these old local photos and landed on his parents' doorstep. It had been kind, he thought, many a one in her position wouldn't have bothered her head. Knowing well, but refusing to admit, that it had been a mistake, that over the phone she'd been confusing him with his brother Brendan, the Redemptorist, who occasionally contributed to Seancais ArdMacha ...

"A series of articles?"

"No, a book actually. Just a popular ... The famine's only part of it. But maybe," he added, feeling the need to make some gesture, some nod of recognition towards her local renown, "maybe you wanted to write about it yourself? I mean I wouldn't want to ... If it's one of your specialities I mean ... "

"Murder's my specialty," she stated causing him to glance up, somewhat startled, and to catch her hard grey indecipherable eyes. "The Claghan massacres. Do you realise that those bogholes out there are thick with the bodies of innocent dead? Young fellows armed with pitchforks and scythes!"

His eyes swivelled to the picture window, to the small spent turf-bog of his boyhood: "I hadn't known," he said, appalled, "I never heard about ... I've been away," he stumbled. "Pitchforks and scythes against Cromwell's Ironsides!" she swept on and he giggled slightly at his own stupidity.

"Well in that case I shan't be trespassing," he smiled, retrieving himself, retrieving his startled eyes from her cold ones, adding with hesitant generosity: "I'm afraid I couldn't write the kind of thing you do anyway. Mine would be more ... "

"And I certainly couldn't write your sort of stuff," she said flatly and, again startled, he met the grey eyes under the grey brows under the grey hair and this time they were decipherable and in them he saw his years of well-intentioned liberalism, his *Statesman* pieces, his *Guardian* pieces, *Observer* pieces, unique volume of short stories, poems in New Irish Writing.

Her brisk voice and unquestioning eyes told him how frivolous were the causes that concerned him, how ephemeral such headline gimmicks as the nuclear threat, apartheid, rights of man, rights of woman, polluted oceans, neo-Nazism, destruction of the planet, in face of the long cruel martyrdom of his native land.

Caricatured in her eyes he even saw the (admittedly frivolous) occasion on which his novel had been conceived. Saw himself at Joanna's parents' house in Hampstead that Sunday before lunch, a group of nice intelligent English socialists with drinks in their hands, himself standing with Joanna's mother being angry about a new sensational book on the North he'd been given to review, ("There's more *to* it, there's always been more to it than all this agony in the Belfast slums! There were other realities and they're getting lost now. There was a wisdom, there was an innocence ... ") and his mother-in-law saying brightly: "But why on earth don't *you* write about Ulster, Owen? Who else is better qualified? A popular novel about Claghan?" He'd laughed and said: "But I left the place a century ago!" and Joanna, whom he hadn't known was listening, turned from the blond sociologist she might or might not be sleeping with and said in a sweet-and-sour voice: "Wrong! You *never* left the place, Owen!"

And as he turned away to the window to digest *that* he

caught sight of his father-in-law swooping and darting down the street like a great foolish bird, squawking noisily back from his ritual Sunday morning visit to the local: university scarf flying, long white strands of his hair flying, Burberry carefully folded inside out flying over one arm, a pocket of his hairy old tweed jacket deformed by a huge tattered copy of *Lord of the Rings*. And he recalled again the wise old men of his childhood pacing in slow measured dignity down the Sunday fields and thought: Yes. Why not? Why not Claghan remembered, by a native son? Claghan venerated? At the same time drinking nourishment from my native roots, he thought, because otherwise what? Otherwise drift on into this pampered liberalism, this élite democracy, this conventional eccentricity, end up a foolish cuckolded old professor like your boyo here, a cliché with long hair and no roots at all and Tolkien sticking out of his pocket. Or in my case Borges, he thought, which has at least the virtue of being less cumbersome. And instantly the image was with him: El campo muerto de hambre, pobre como una araña. A starting point. Yes.

"Why not?" he said, "Yes why not, after all. I think I'll pop back over there when term ends, spend a month or so interrogating the 'wise old men'." Taking care to shelter them inside inverted commas from the possibility of alien mockery.

"Back to Eden," Joanna laughed, "where the opposite of right is wrong, not left."

And her trendy sociologist added: "Where gay still means gay. And not gay."

Joanna's mother, who had been brought up a Catholic, chimed in: "Where the family that prays together preys together."

While he began to finger once again the decent well-worn beads of his private rosary: Bob Maguire, Jamesy Murphy, Ned Maginn, the bog, the kesh, the dusty street, the pighouse under the sycamore trees ... But the old men were dead.

"We'll *all* be dead," the historian said, "before this book gets written."

He read his history in her grudging small-town eyes: country gawk, dropout, reformed junkie, superannuated hippie, spineless bastard who took the first plane out, leaving the old men to die with their memories.

And of course she is right, he thought with whipped humility after she'd gone, but then what much better did she do? What better did any of them do that stayed? They collected folksongs, it's true, wrote about forgotten massacres, unearthed an old Mass-rock, restored the tombstones in Claghan graveyard (Gaelic nobles, minor landlords and eighteenth-century poets) but they couldn't stop the blight spreading all the same could they? he thought, watching camouflage uniforms slinking up under the hawthorns, up dead Maginn's shrunken field. And the children who died in every generation in that pighouse didn't *have* tombstones to restore, they died and were buried anonymously. Yes but their memorial is the Armalite rifle, he was told, we kill that they may have eternal life ...

And if the Maguires had been left in their castles, he thought, if the Wild Geese hadn't spread a crafty wing on every tide, we could have blamed them for the famine, dragged them to their deaths in tumbrels or in their own magnificent carriages, escorted by the bleeding ghosts of serfs and bondsmen and ruined shopkeepers and weeping widows and starving peasants back to the dawn of history.

Oh, we'd have done it, he thought, we'd have been fit to do it all right. Going about here and there borrowing documents, asking questions, recording answers (coffin-ships, blight, internment, Tans, Bloody Sunday), examining in bewilderment the shrunken invaded meadows of his boyhood. Recalling slow old men pacing with measured steps down his father's field on a Sunday after Mass, missals in their coat pockets, wise old men in the state of grace puffing out pipe smoke fragrant as hawthorn, puffing out wise measured statements about a century-old genocide. El campo muerto de hambre, pobre como una araña. ("Talking some old rubbidge of nonsense like the rest of us!" his father jeered, "Sure you were only a wee child, how could you have knew what they were talking about?")

He used to sit on the big stone behind the pighouse in the sun, watching them pacing down in the shadows of the hawthorn, knowledge slowly growing in him that the nearest you could ever approach to his dream of flying, to the ownership of fields and clouds and air, was to be an old man in the state of grace with Sunday in your pocket, moving with measured steps down a scented hedgerow talking slow wisdom. It came to him now that he possibly could not have heard what they were saying, that he might have grafted on to their slow nodding heads statements overheard at other times, in other places, perhaps even from other slow old men in other martyred countries. (Perhaps merely read, in some schoolteacher's articles.)

"I see you're home," they told him when he walked into a shop that existed unchanged since his childhood. "Doing anything exciting?"

"I'm sitting in a deck-chair on the site of my father's old pighouse trying to make head or tail of a line out of Borges." "I'm researching a book about the famine." "I'm in danger of getting tangled up in a web of lying memories." Three statements to raise an eyebrow or a cheer, so he answered instead: "I'm buying a pound of rashers for my mother," and they laughed but (perhaps?) not with him.

Their jeering grudging eyes spied on him as, he recalled, they always had jeeringly spied, raking him from head to toe for visible signs of success and not finding any.

"That wee Oweny fella has no ambition," used to be the judgement and there was no reason, he supposed, why it should have altered. He didn't own a car and even if he'd carried his shabby old raincoat inside out, (which he was always careful not to do, out of a personal refinement of snobbery) they would be unlikely to recognise it as a badge, however anxiety-ridden, of status. He was thin and city-pale and balding, his marriage was less than perfect, he'd bought his trousers from an Oxfam shop five years earlier. (Another tribal scar, but they wouldn't recognise that either.) He suspected that they were patriotically ashamed of him, and humanly glad of the chance to be so. *He* could bring them no credit, sitting in a deck chair reading poetry as years ago he'd lain eccentric and friendless in long meadow grass while they kicked football, stunted wee bawky of a thing out of a zinc-roofed shack making up some foolishness round a few broken jyes of delf turned up by the old men's plough. *He* was not the native son who would ever cause this place to be mentioned with veneration.

The shopkeeper, a contemporary of his, had spent two years in the Maze prison. "I wouldn't recommend it," he smiled, heroically laconic. His younger brother, he said, was running in marathons all over the place, the States and everywhere, trying to raise money for a Community Centre. A former teacher, fine footballer too in his day, was contributing articles on local folk-music to *Ireland's Own*. Great things were being done for Claghan's old, unemployed, handicapped.

They were useful people, respected people, and they knew it, secure in the encircling arms of their country, of this town so rich in history, in armed resistance, in righteous violent death. He admired them. One had to. To spend two years in a prison camp and come out smiling! Unmarked? Hardly. Perhaps enriched, perhaps diminished, but certainly possessing some quiet sure knowledge of oneself that he, now, was unlikely ever to attain. The knowledge of themselves that those old men had attained – worn fine by labour, by hunger, by prayer, by an inbred awareness of their race's martyrdom? But he was wounded by these people, as he always had been, and conscious as he always had been that he was shamefully lacking in even the smallest of their certainties.

Only what do they find so contemptible, he wondered (rebelling as he always had rebelled, once escaped from the web of their eyes). What's so contemptible about me (serious and hardworking as I am in spite of everything) sitting for the space of a summer holiday on this flowering terrace where a pighouse used to stand, where a few scraggy hens used to peck anxiously at the street's hungry dust? Am I not their equal now after all?

But he recalled Claghan primary school in the early fifties, the big sturdy shopkeepers' sons, publicans' sons, cattle dealers' sons with their pockets full of dainties, openly munching their way through Sharps toffees, red bought apples, Custard Creams, under the begging complaining eyes of the barefoot stirabout boys from the five-acre farms.

Owen stole an orange one fair day, hid it all weekend in the sycamore tree, went to Communion on Sunday with the sin on his soul, thinking damnation well worth while because he would at last on Monday achieve equality. He opened his schoolbag at milk time, drew out the orange with rehearsed casualness, peeled it, and sank his teeth in the winy juice, casually taking his place among the privileged. Waiting like the privileged for the cajoling whisper: "Gis a bite! Gwan, gis a lump Owen!" Instead, someone called: "Would yous look at wee Oweny suckin away at his wee wizened orange!", and in the wild storm of cheers that followed he saw himself reflected ridiculously in their eyes, a puny barefoot boy in a man's cut-down suit, sucking at a stolen orange like a rat sucking an egg, and saw the presumption of ever taking himself for their equal.

But *why*, he'd thought then, why this need to see myself reflected in *their* eyes? I have parents who love me, brothers and sisters, I'm the first in the class, shouldn't that be enough? And now he thought: why aren't the eyes of my friends enough, my wife's eyes, the accepting eyes of my colleagues? Why aren't my pay-cheques enough, my work for human rights, my pretty house, my holidays in France and Italy, my place securely hollowed out in a world that's more evolved, after all, than this one? After twenty years who do I still feel that I've only left Claghan temporarily, that I'm only lent out on an extended visit to Life? Why the need to return here, to be witnessed by them praying at Mass-rocks, hoking about in graveyards, venerating the ignorant skeletons of old men? Get away, get away, he thought. Cut yourself free before they destroy your home, your marriage, the few small realities you own. Before they destroy *you*.

Joanna's roots and the roots of the blond sociologist she might or might not be in love with were torn up decades ago to make way for an Underground railway line. They had nowhere to go back to. They could only go forwards and outwards. They had no eyes to search for their reflections in except their own. And each others'. The spiteful slum eyes that might have imprisoned them or diminished them were scattered long ago, forgotten and nameless, all over London. (Only then, why did his father-in-law feel the need on a Sunday morning to walk out of a warm comfortable house full of alcohol and good talk and stand drinking in a workman's pub in West Hampstead, flaunting like decorations the fading status symbols of his generation? For whose eyes?)

A Novel about the Famine

"Pay no heed to that jumped-up crowd," his father said, "Big shots aye! Sure I used to know that fella's father when he was selling herrings off a barrow!" Which was hardly the point either, Owen thought, but said nothing.

His mother, glad to have him home, to have him quietly going here and there among neighbours, apparently cured of his old rages and rovings and discontents, fed him tea and sweet biscuits, sent love over the phone to Joanna, recounted local scandals in a dramatic whisper: the shocking goings-on in the housing estate, wife-swapping and drugs and God knows what, and wee children running about that even their own mothers didn't know who owned them; awful times, desperate times son! But she seemed to be taking it in her stride, as she had apparently taken in her stride the town's slow change from friendly primitive place (last outpost of a traditional Gaelic lifestyle, they said when they restored the graveyard) to scene of intermittent slaughter. "Joanna didn't come over," he apologised. "She didn't like to, being English ... "

"Och she'd have been in no danger," his father said. "Sure she has no one belonging to her in the army has she?"

His father was approaching the age of the wise old men but he sat among his tubs of roses reading gardening magazines and jotting down tips for making compost – he who'd raised a family on five boggy acres, who'd lived for thirty years in the shadow of a steaming dunghill. Owen found him easier to deal with, coaxed him into anecdotes of the past. His father told how big Ned Maginn had borrowed a wooden rake from him thirty years ago, refused to return it, denied ever borrowing it; how he, ashamed to give the lie to the old man but badly needing the rake, was obliged to creep up the field late one night and steal his property out of Maginn's shed; how old Maginn a few nights later stole it back again; how this continued for years, neither giving in, neither letting on; meeting civilly every day of their lives, creeping up and down the field at night till in the long run nobody knew right who the old rake belonged to. "Oh a mean old blaggard Ned!" And all the time, Owen thought, big Ned Maginn was walking down that headland of a Sunday, puffing with slow quiet wisdom at his clay pipe, his sage old head nodding, a wise old man in the state of grace ...

And if my old men were not saints, he wondered, or martyrs? Or even wise? If they had no deep knowledge of themselves, or of life? If they were just blowing out empty remembered slogans blindly invented in some windowless pighouse? (If they were talking about something else altogether, some local thing, a neighbour's failure, a stolen rake?) If they were only tired trapped people wriggling feebly with no real hope, and no real wish, to break free from the web this country endlessly, tirelessly, spins? What wealth has a spider only its web?

"I mightn't know much about the famine," his father said, "but bejaiburs I could tell you plenty about th'oul' playboys used to be in these townlands. Do you know what I'm going to tell you son, there was some of the greatest bleddy rascals ... God forgive me for talking bad of the people! Mind you there was decent men too. Reb and Callan and Mick Morris and poor Paddy lord a mercy on him, but there was a lot of oul' meanness among the people long ago, oh aye! Did y'ever hear tell of the time poor Bayonets Bogan found the treasure in the boghole? Well it was ... "

Owen thought of those heroic old men and women creeping to the Mass-rock through eighteenth-century Penal darkness, and imagined them spying on one another, as they surely did, with the same grudging gossiping eyes as the people in that shop. And did the first field to be hit by blight, he wondered, raise a few cackles of spiteful

A Novel about the Famine

laughter ("Sure I knew as soon as I seen the cut of yon fella diggin his drills! Not one of that breed ever ... ")?

And if it hadn't been unanimous, he wondered, if there had been some who hadn't wanted to go to that Mass-rock? Some who were convinced otherwise, some who had doubts, who were groping their way towards another kind of certainty, who had wider horizons? Some who wouldn't necessarily have thought it a betrayal to accept the Protestant minister's well-intentioned bowl of soup? Don't forget your other granda, he thought, who discarded his faith, came back from England a man of fifty with the clothes on his back, a trunk full of books, and a cracked harmless philosophy to live by: remember how the neighbours gathered round his house that first Sunday and how a crowd of them went in to Claghan and took out the missionary to him?

And if in reality nobody had wanted to creep to the Mass-rock? If it was all a cod? If they'd one and all been helpless in a web spun by a small town's spying eyes? Helpless yes, he thought, but well protected by the web too, as they still are protected. Protected from doubt, from having to ask questions of themselves, from having to make any but the most superficial of choices? Proud to be seen standing unyielding in its grip while the flesh is slowly eaten off their unyielding bones. There are other kinds of famine.

He pictured the heroes and victims, the teachers and priests and social workers and local historians, stuck in a web whose strangling grip so woundingly, so dangerously, resembled a warm accepting embrace to those who were safe outside it. A country dead of hunger, poor as a spider, he thought (a small child whimpering in his heart telling him he was safe outside it.) Safe and despised in a deck chair reading poetry. Safe in his treacherous awareness that the fields below the terrace had not shrunk, that they always had been that narrow web criss-crossed with confining hedges.

"Oul' rascals!" his father said, "The wee-est wee thing a body ever done there'd always be some neighbour to make little of it."

Safe, but perhaps it was too late to be safe?

"Lawsuits and ructions and families that didn't speak from one generation to the next. We were all in a poor way of going, but do you know what it is Owen, there was some of them playboys would take the eye out of your head if they thought they could make tuppence on it!"

Was it too late to be safe?

"I'm going in for a minute," he said, "to ring Joanna. I might get her to come over for a day or two and then I think maybe we'd take a wee run over to France for the rest of the holidays."

"Isn't it well for you?" his father said. "You couldn't go nowhere in my day. Or if you did you carried this bleddy place with you. Over to Scotland for the spuds or the Liverpool docks, it was all one, there was always a pack of oul' Claghaners stuck to you! You were wiser," he said. "You got to hell out of it and you didn't give a damn what anyone thought. Me or your mother or anyone. You were a hard-natured blaggard Owen, and I'd rather not know what devilment you got up to, but do you know what it is … "

The old men are dead, Owen thought, (dialling his London number) and this thing that I'm living in is my future. This is the future that I used to look forward to sitting on that big stone behind the pighouse, the future when I thought I'd be a grown man walking in a field with wisdom in my pocket. This is it and it's half over and I didn't recognise it. I *don't* recognise it. Where are my fields, he wondered, (listening to the phone ringing on and on and on), have I left it too late? Are my fields anywhere now?

His father paced slowly down to the kesh leaving idle blobs of pipe smoke behind on the air, a gardening magazine sticking up out of his pocket. He looked old and frail and very wise. A soldier in Maginn's field stared at him without expression across the kesh, then opened his fly and pissed deliberately into the water. His father stopped, cleared his throat and spat, without expression, dirtily unto the meadow grass.

Is there any wisdom to arrive at, Owen wondered, in Claghan or out of it? And what web is it *I'm* caught in?

Beggars Upon Horseback

"Heavenly house!" Climbing flight after polished flight, sliding across the bedroom parquets. "Oh the big tall windows! Oh the painted ceilings!" Park outside falling away down to the wood, ornamental moat smothered in briars (but that could be seen to), small white houses shining away above the treetops, two slim spires: "Heavenly village!"

"Well there's no need to go all Nancy Mitford," he crushed.

"I was doing it deliberately," Brigid said. "Not much sense of humour have you? D'you think I'm taking all this seriously? Lady of the Manor do you think I'm thinking? I mean I'm aware we're not *buying* the place, just moving in for a year or two with our whitewood furniture. Like in a squat autrefois, only paying rent. Like real adults. I mean we used to squat in places just as grand as this, didn't we? Will you ever forget Maastricht and the Kastel Burgh? But the darling wee farmhouse! We'll be able to buy milk and free-range eggs. Look, oh look, Pierre, a red-cheeked fermière in sabots, isn't it fantastic, isn't it *French*!"

"Oh look," he sneered, "a Mercedes in the farmyard, and a BMW. Never heard of this crowd did you? Never watch the News? Spend their weekends burning lorry-loads of English lamb at the docks, Irish butter, the lot. Look at that fat guy, the farmer, he's got a Cardin label on his dungarees."

"Haha very funny, you have great eyes."

"Not eyes. Vision. It's their country now. Places like this, the old landlady and that, they're all washed up these days. Bloody good job too!"

And ran downstairs chanting: "No more massa's lash for me/Ole cat's got at the cream-oh!"

"Ha, and again ha, very funny."

She brought the children to the village school, shortcutting with them through the woods, chestnut she recognised and beech, and later on they could come of a Sunday to pick fraises de bois, and then five minutes stroll up a narrow hedged road to the école laique. Carloads of satchelled children vsst! vsst! doing a hundred round the perilous bends, no one offered her a lift. Two Mercedes she counted, four BMWs, the rest big fat Peugeots, Pierre must be right. Ah no, there's a wee Renault 5 all beat-up and ancient, ouf! the relief of it. And one other woman walking, drearily. Not, you could see, like Brigid, not walking for the joy of it, just slogging away day after day with two dim-looking daughters. No one offered her a lift either.

Brigid bought croissants every morning in the village store, carton of UHT ("Sorry Madame, we have to sell all our milk to the Creamery nowadays." He didn't have a Cardin label but he did wear Dior sunglasses and his wife's clogs were Scandinavian. As indeed was his wife.) She drank mugs of café au lait, waxed the parquet floors, took a slash-hook to the briars, lived for a while in an enchantment of woods and flowers and ease of her lovely old house. She got a few smiles at the school gate, her daughters made friends, though only with the dim-looking walkers. The walking woman spoke to her sometimes, was even waiting for her sometimes as she emerged from the dark of the woods. Madame Lemoine. Spoke badly, dressed badly, occasionally her words were oddly slurred, her tired Madonna face oddly smeared with cheap makeup: "Got my warpaint on to go shopping in Plancoet." She was a slight embarrassment, what could one possibly say to her, but at least she was cheerful and the road short.

The landlady called, was shocked about the village school, said but why don't you send them to the Convent? Said your children are being taught by the daughter of my cook. Said they teach Communist propaganda in these State schools, didn't you know? Said it's a well-known fact, Madame, that all the May '68 rioters are now heads of primary schools corrupting our innocent youth. She spoke of her tenant farmers, said Monsieur Vitel down the hill was a dangerous left-wing agitator.

"Not possible! What, with his Dior specs and all?"

"Quand même, quand même Madame, I know what I'm talking about. All through the last election campaign he carried a bunch of red roses on his tractor. So insolent!"

"Insolent indeed," Brigid agreed, "but did they not cut off his ears with the garden shears and bring them to you in a little silver dish?"

The old countess reeled back, pale, hearing the babble of a mad revolutionary, her poor old ears suddenly deafened with a rumble of approaching tumbrels.

"It's all right," Brigid soothed, "a quotation. Yeats you know."

"Ah yes of course. Your Irish Shakespeare. 'I must have men about me that are fat.' My English governess used to say that, then we all assumed that was why she eloped with a Vitel. Actually we could never understand why she found it necessary to elope: it was the tradition for centuries that our governesses married the tenant farmers.

Take the Vitels now, they've been in our family for three hundred years and they're simply riddled with Swiss, Scotch, German, even an émigrée Russian princess. But of course the English are an eccentric people. They would like to kill me, you know."

"The English?"

"The Vitels. They will kill me, they will kill us all. It is not enough for them that I am no longer mayor of the village, that I have had to let my château to foreigners and live in a cottage, that I am crushed by taxes, no, in the end they will come and kill me."

Brigid said no of course they wouldn't, how unlikely: old Uncle Mitterand wasn't going to last forever, and anyhow Socialist revolution works differently, she said, words like 'redistribution' yes but gently, not I mean, tac-tac-tac Kalashnikov and that, she said, no it's more well I mean, they'd probably more want to marry your daughters wouldn't they?"

"*That* would kill me, Madame!" And the landlady stalked out. Oh dear-a-dear.

One morning, walking all Thoreau-ly through the lovely woods, Brigid, swooning up at the new pale leaves, put her foot down on a mess of blood and feathers. Yuk, wood pigeon disembowelled, dis-indeed-everything. Of course, of course she might have known, lovely woods oh yeah, things eating each other, things lurking and pouncing and tearing. Owls and weasels and stoats. In the night unearthly screeches. The ornamental moat a place of chronic slaughter. Moles too, not nice upperclass gents in velvet suits shacked up with gay water-rats, not at all; worming away for all they were worth, just look at the state of the lawn, lupins cowped over in the flowerbeds. As Spring progressed she found herself obliged to put down poison in their tunnels, set rat traps in outhouses. On walks she began to be aware of more and more small dead things, fledglings smashed, shells unsnailed. Ulysses, her cat, roamed far afield, returned every morning gorged and sickened with field mice. In the night from hedge and wood screams of panic drifted through her open windows. A filmy top layer was peeled almost imperceptibly off the enchantment of her life.

Much remained. The trees and the neighbours' smiles and the big tall rooms to walk through, cool dimness as she plunged into the wood. As long as you watch your step, she thought, keep the moles off the lawn, weasels out of the chicken-run, get the housework done at dawn in case of stray callers. But no one called except the old landlady mourning for her vanished world. Brigid walked twice daily between the lines of parked cars at the school gate, and the women went no further than smiles. They called to one another from car to car and she was apart. Not apart like poor Madame Lemoine at whom nobody smiled, but apart. She began to feel that they were testing her, waiting for her to make a false move, watching to see in what mess she would put down her foot.

Her daughters came home crying: "They say if we play with Odette Lemoine no one else will ever want to play with us."

"Who say?"

"All the others, the Vitels and them. She has nits they say, and her sister too. Odette and Claudine they're dirty girls and they're poor and they have nits, maman!"

"And what if they have? And then anyway you've been playing with them for months and how many nits did you catch? Play away as much as you like with them, who's the Vitels to give orders?"

You can always, she thought, run to the chemist, buy a tin of Parapoux, pschitt! pschitt! clean heads, but once you start making snobs of them ...

And again: "Maman," they asked, "why don't you take

us to school in the car? Michèle Bude wasn't friends with us yesterday and she said we couldn't afford the petrol that was why. She said we were broke. And everyone said. Vos parents sont des fauchés, they said. And Maman why haven't we two cars, everyone has two cars?"

"Your friend Odette hasn't."

"Odette bee-urk! Odette has nits instead." The two small girls nudged each other, giggling hysterically: "She has nits instead, she rides to school on her nits, Maman!"

Brigid drew out and slapped them, hard. "In the car, are you daft or what? Five minutes walk through the woods, if we took the car we'd have to go right round by the bridge, five kilometres at the very least do you realise?"

"The Vitels live nearer than us and they – "

"It'd fit the Vitels better to walk, might melt some of the lard off them. The Vitels are nothing, do you hear, nothing! Why a few years ago they were only serfs, at the beck and call of our landlady."

So fare-you-well to tolerance. Another thin layer of enchantment peeled off her life as she walked, less proudly, out of the wood.

Madame Lemoine was waiting for her, green eyelids, auburn rinse, all smiles: "Why don't you come and see me some day, bring the children, come and have a coffee."

"I will, oh I will." Taken aback she was over-enthusiastic: God what have I let myself in for now, she thought. "After the school fête. Some Saturday." Only why encourage her like that? Was this to be the bosom friend of her heavenly new life?

"Are you helping at the fête?" she asked.

"You're joking, Madame? I'm not even going. Never been to their fête, it's not for the like of you and me, all that! They wouldn't throw a word to you, any of those high-ups. Farmers and typists and bank clerks, too much money they have! I'll bet they didn't ask you either."

"Actually they did," Brigid said coldly. "The headmistress asked. I'm supposed to be helping at the coffee stall with Madame Vitel and the dentist's wife."

Likes of you and me indeed!

The Parents' Association met on a Friday to prepare for the fête, roll up, roll up, all welcome, bring old newspapers to wrap the Lucky Dips. *Ouest France*, *Le Monde*, and the dentist's wife brought a stack of *Nouvel Observateurs*, too glossy to be of any use. Bonsoir Madame, bonsoir Madame, bonsoir Madame: they came in family groups, neighbour groups, income groups. They had all been to the hairdresser. Water pistols were priced, prizes wrapped, cellophane bags filled (five toffees, two Carambars, a Chiclet). Group to one side, group to the other, Brigid in the middle feeling naked. Trying her best: "Come here often?" Yes Madame, no Madame, frozen smiles. What do I have to do for godsake! how many years live here? She filled another sack and another and another. In shy silence, boredom, embarrassment, flittered through the pile of newspapers, read the cartoons, trying to give herself a countenance.

"Madame? Oh Madame! All alone? Do come and sit with us."

The headmistress, the cook's daughter, the poor landlady's communist. Abject with gratitude Brigid smiled, laughed, chattered at the teachers' table. Questioned and was questioned. Who's so-and-so? Really? And have you lived here long Madame? Oh and that woman, she asked, Madame Lemoine, I don't see her here, who is she exactly? The headmistress looked suddenly worried: "Oh Madame I'm sorry about that, her daughters do insist on playing with yours, I've tried to drop a gentle hint but apparently ... Would you like me to say something, put my foot down?"

"Why? Why? What do you mean, foot down?" Too emphatically.

They looked at her with prim startled faces. "Oh a dreadful family, Madame. The limit! Six of them in one room – "

"In one *bed*!" giggled the dentist's wife. "He's been on the sick for years. Sick with red wine more likely. And she's a bit defective you know, oh I don't mean mental but she just can't cope, have you seen the way those girls are dressed, ghastly bright colours from second-hand shops, they could catch *anything*!"

"Oh she can cope all right when it comes to claiming free lunches and welfare!" the headmistress said, "And they say he *beats* her."

"It's the kids I feel sorry for actually," said Madame Vitel, "but what can one do? It's no good encouraging them, we have our own to think of. Nits. Bad language. Best to leave them alone really. And she's expecting another."

"Rabbits!" giggled the dentist's wife, "Pure rabbits!" Her small pretty face was sparkling, "And listen, they say *she* drinks too. Imagine!"

"Well *I'd* drink," Brigid interrupted, "if I had to live like that. I expect it's just no one's bothered to tell her about Valium. Imagine a whole family having to live in one room in a socialist country, and goodness when you think how your papers keep on and on about Thatcher's Britain! Anyhow she invited me round for a coffee which is more than anyone else bothered to do in the six months I've been here!"

The headmistress clapped her hands loudly: "Oh no! Listen to this, everyone, just listen. That Lemoine woman only had the cheek to invite Madame, the Irish lady, to drop in for a coffee. Did you ever?" "Drop in for a glass of vin rouge you mean!" "Oh don't go, Madame, you mustn't even think of going there! Quel horreur!" The room thawed into one pool of giggles. Pointed little teeth nicely capped, varnished heads tossed elegantly back, ripple of fine gold earrings. Small squeaks and whirls and yelps of méchant pretty laughter welcoming Brigid in out of the cold ...

" ... So how was the meeting? They invite you to join the Mother's Union?" Half-asleep jeer, not really interested. She shook him awake: "My God, Pierre such a right crowd of bitches, just listen till I tell you – "

"Oh Christ woman not *now*! It's the middle of the night. Tell us all about it in the morning eh?" Heave of blankets. Exaggerated snores.

She lay awake, planning, planning. Tomorrow, yes first thing tomorrow afternoon, I'll go round there. Bunch of flowers from the garden, yes and buy a cake. No, bake one, make the effort, let her see ... (And if she's drunk? If her old man gets violent? If they insist on pouring you a glass of that filthy red vinegar they probably drink? Insult you? Come out with some dirty talk?) Oh for godsake Brigid be your *age*, you're not a child now! Coax, persuade, drag her by force to the fête. Buy a toy for the kids. (Six toys, remember?) Sit down and have coffee with her in front of everyone, make the dentist's wife serve it, yeah. (But will I ever have the courage?) And that Madame Vitel, self-righteous cow, jumped-up foreign nanny wouldn't you know, backside like a bloody Volvo, and the accent! Shpitting and shpluttering. (But she's my nearest neighbour: I can't afford to ...)

She remembered old Phelimy Oates years ago in his tin-roofed shack in the middle of Maginn's field – drew his pension of a Friday, had it drunk by Saturday night – and how every evening after school she and her brothers were sent over with a can of milk, cake of bread, bit of liver if there was a pig-killing: "Above all don't let yous just hand him the few things and run; let yous sit down with the poor man and make a bit of a visit. And if he offers yous tea, take it!" Sometimes he offered gooseberries off the bushes in front of his door and, though you knew he regularly stood in that doorway and pissed blindly over them, you took them anyway out of courtesy, filled your pockets with them: "I'll take them home to share with the wee ones, Phelimy, and thanks." Once out of sight you flung them away in the briars, washed your hands in the stream. Sometimes her mother or father went with the food themselves, sat and chatted like neighbours though it must, she realised now, have been agony for them, holy and teetotal as they were and aware, as they were, that coming up on the Fair Day Phelimy harboured any old trash that walked the roads (though her parents, unlike most, never said 'old trash'; they said 'unfortunate poor creatures God forgive them'.) She recalled how, that winter Sunday, before the coffin lid was right nailed down, Ned Maginn sent in a bulldozer to demolish Phelimy's home and how her two young brothers camped the whole morning on Bogan's Rock with a heap of stones and pelted Maginn's workmen so that they were forced to retreat and leave the old shack decently standing till after the funeral.

Yes but her parents had nothing to prove. They were in their own place, well thought of, admired; they had their way made. She envied them for an instant, at home there with their feet firmly on the ground, belonging to themselves, impervious to praise or blame, doing their Christian duty gracefully without question or hesitation. She remembered her own disgusted boredom sitting on a stool in Phelimy's shack pretending to drink tea out of a filthy chipped cup, swiftly splashing it behind the fire if he once turned his back: the hiss, the stink of wet ashes that he must surely have noticed. She regretted that she hadn't been up there on Bogan's rock with the boys that day. Where *had* she been? Stuck in some corner no doubt, as usual, dreaming with her nose in a book, letting

Chimborazi Cotopaxi steal her heart away – when reality was being camped heroically on the top of a rock pegging stones at hired men. As reality still was ...

Hurrah for revolution, she thought, her mind spinning with anxiety. Stones she ought to have pegged, remarks she ought to have made, staircase wit that would have demolished them. Shower of jumped-up peasants. As the landlady would say. *Did* say over and over, her place for the moment usurped, the lash for the moment in other hands. And Brigid in the middle, anxious with guilt.

Presumably her two brothers were free of any guilt about old Phelimy. Guilt over those exchanged grimaces when his back was turned courteously wiping a dirty cup with a dirty dishcloth. Guilt that in spite of all the neighbourliness he had never felt free to stroll down to their house of an evening, (subtler guilt at the assumption that he would have *wanted* to). Guilt that she had carefully never been allowed to meet any of the tramps and prostitutes and gypsy singers who sheltered in his shack when there was a Fair in the town. That on Fair evenings in fact he didn't get his can of milk and his cake of soda bread. That in the long run, cut off from the road in a terrible blizzard, he died alone without a fire and was discovered days later chewed up by rats. What can you do for anyone, she wondered, if you don't do everything?

She lay awake, seeing herself friendless in a strange place, condemned to make her choice. Either everlasting guilt or everlasting intimacy with poor gabbling drunken Madame Lemoine; herself catalogued for life, cut off from any hope of other friendships, her children woundingly labelled, excluded from the smiles and the fêtes and the laughter.

For hours she lay awake listening to the merciless night. Small squeaks and whirls and yelps. Thin shrieks of terror, of triumph, a snapping of neat little teeth, an owl's screech. The beautiful countryside pouncing and savaging and tearing itself. Tomorrow just another mess for her to step in. And no enchantment left at all.

An Exorcism

Eve, in exile, sat aimlessly by a tall open window watching the sun slithering about on the slope of grass, the beech tree frozen helplessly into a posture eternally awaiting some signal to go leaping headlong down the hill to join its colleagues in the wood. She was conscious of her baby asleep in the next room, the door ajar. Of her husband somewhere up above, typing. She had nothing whatsoever to do. Her notebook lay open on the table but she was incapable of writing another word. She had already put down two sentences, re-read them, and been sickened by their banality.

She knew that she was in for one of those periods of aridity that came to her more or less frequently and whose onset was characterised by the recurrence of a depressing little fantasy in which any one of her favourite writers should be stranded at an Irish airport, should buy an Irish paper, should let his eyes lap languidly at a few lines of one of her stories and then, without the slightest change of expression, should quietly turn over to the racing page. This fantasy was situated so far inside the frontier of possibility (Graham Greene, of course, didn't get around so much anymore but supposing Naipaul, en route for South

America, should be obliged to change planes at Shannon?) that it was continually stopping her dead in her tracks, making her shove notebook and felt pen away in the landing cupboard and direct all her creative energy towards knitting Aran ganseys for the children. So that often, needing a pen to write a grocery list, she was forced to burrow and scrabble in the depths of the press. There they all were, buried in lavender, among the scented towels and the wedding-present sheets.

She was aware that the pessimistic nature of this fantasy was a direct result of having begun to write at the ripe old age of thirty-five. Had she started at nineteen her imaginings might have been other. (The seated figure in the departure lounge suddenly clenching itself into a position of intense excitement; exclaiming: "Mein Gott!" or "Yikes!" or "Caramba!", rushing off to Dublin to see the editor, seeking her out in her picturesque attic room: "Comrade! Comrade!" What Adam called the Mills and Boon corner of her mind.)

But she was now thirty-nine, had long abandoned homeland and attic, had published twelve stories and two dozen articles, and no doubt in the meantime a succession of distinguished voyagers had touched down at Shannon, booked in at the Gresham, had a few jars with Seamus Heaney – and endlessly turned the page to see what won the three-thirty.

Her sitting-room was panelled in old-rose, the tall narrow windows looked out in three directions. She leaned forward to smile at a farmer's wife driving cows down the lane to the field. The woman did not respond, looked briefly up at her and turned aside. Eve went to the table and wrote quickly: "Rejection slips broad-rumped into my life, shaped like a dour countrywoman smelling faintly of cow dung, driving her own cattle to her own acres, returning smug to the security of her own four solid walls.

Sensing that I am one of those who pay weekly rent to the Unknown, aware of the fragility of my tenure, my absence of guarantees, she turns away fearing to compromise her immortality by acknowledging me." She re-read the paragraph over a grey-flannel shoulder in an airport lounge. No good. Clever-clever, that's all I am, she thought, the pretentious good child that keeps on winning scholarships.

She walked into the next room and bent over her baby dreaming. That ought to be enough, surely that ought to suffice? The ultimate act of creation, repeated four times. And of course it did usually suffice, her life did suffice. She was a reasonably happy lady, she reflected, perched there precariously on a hilltop, in her lovely rented house with the woods at her feet, her children playing or dreaming or screaming around her. Joseph Conrad, she'd been told at college, never stopped whingeing because he was obliged to hear through a thin bedroom wall the breathing of his sick child, while he was trying to write. By those standards she was no Conrad. The best that could happen to her now was "Housewife Writes Bestseller." And the worst: Hardy's Imaginative Woman.

Surely, between the two, there was some serene place where she could live respected by herself, the many facets and colours of her existence finally fitted together to form the kaleidoscope that was Eve? It was not even necessary to be a creator. If my own eyes are blinded, she thought, won't I be able to see just as well through the eyes of my enlightened brothers? "Si me quitaron los ojos," she hummed to the sleeping baby, "lo mismo he de verlo yo, Con los ojos de ... " De Joyce, de Sartre, de Beethoven, de. Even if I did nothing but stand in front of my wide-open windows and see out wouldn't that have some value?

"Well would yous listen to *her*!" she jeered suddenly, assuming a cynical Belfast accent, "I fear thon wee woman

An Exorcism

thinks she's the Lady of Shallot!"

Grabbing notebook and pen she marched out to the landing cupboard. At that moment the doctor's car stopped on the gravel outside.

Anna Moreau rang the bell and waited. Her pale mild eyes slid over the paintwork, the slope of lawn, over Eve running down past the landing window; made a quick diagnosis, registered: "Foreigner." Her feet were solid in Breton clogs, her legs slightly bowed in green tights, her skirt chintz like an English armchair. Eve, letting her in, was puzzled at the small ashamed awareness between them of her own pleated polyester dress, quite clean and decent, but bought long ago in some absent-minded hurry. She had lost the habit of other women's company. "Oh no, of course you're not! Do please come in."

"I have been to Ireland, you know." Anna Moreau was sitting, mild-eyed and gentle in the rose-coloured room, speaking careful English. "Not touristique! Not with a guide! We take sacks on our back, my fiancé and me last summer and forever we are sleeping in the huts of poor peasants. In Connemara. Always we share their lives, of these simple people, we are eating the same food. So natural they are and friendly, the human warmth we encounter always."

Eve smiled and did not know what to say.

"I shall not be forgetting that country so quick! But today I come on another business. I am, as you say, publicising for our little movement of human rights. You have heard of us perhaps? It interests you, the human rights?"

Eve nodded. She had her wild enthusiasms, was at times caught up by the scruff of the neck and shaken sick with the sorrow and the pity. Occasionally, like everyone else, she forced herself to the edge and looked over into terror, returning like everyone else, dizzy with the knowledge of her own helplessness. She nodded.

"Well what I try to publicise, we organise a fête you know? If you care to come and help. It is to show our solidarity with the peasants of El Salvador, is a very good cause," Anna Moreau said. "We would like to have many people. Of course it is not such a popular thing, I mean one cannot expect ... It would not be realistic, I think, to approach the villagers, I do not envisage to take a public collection. We are not the foreign missions after all!" she laughed. "But a few people like us you know, we are informed n'est ce pas, we cannot just sit. You shall tell your friends? And the professors, perhaps, your husband's colleagues? Afterwards, in the evening, we will eat a little supper, with only Salvadorian food. It shall be very authentic and some of, how you say, my pals, they play music."

Eve, caged in the room, saw it all quite clearly: the folk-dancing, the boozy bearded singers, the élite heartiness. Afterwards no doubt a little poetry reading and then Anna Moreau, disguised in poncho and sombrero, passing round plates of ... of *what*, possibly?

"Some simple rice dishes and, I think, a speciality, bananas au poivre, something like that ... " Eve was never quite sure whether Anna Moreau had actually uttered that or whether she herself had only pictured her uttering it in her caricatural English but in any case the whole idea was there in front of her, grotesque and, when you examined it closely, unbelievably disgusting. Pretty coloured leaves floating and dancing on all that blood.

The baby woke and cried. Eve, fetching him, soothing him, seating him on her lap, said quickly: "It's hard to get out anywhere just now ... four children ... I'd rather, really rather not promise anything you see, might have to let you down at the last minute. I'd have loved to help but ... " Anna Moreau said gently that she quite understood but

An Exorcism

wasn't it terrible that Eve couldn't take a day off when she felt like it and wasn't life hard on mothers? Eve, loathing her, snapped: "Yeah we suffer in their coming and their going don't we?" and Anna Moreau said: "What a beautiful thought, almost poetical. But how sad it is and how very very true!" And then Eve, relenting, added: "Oh I suppose eventually we'll find a baby-sitter but just at the moment ... And then not being able to ask a neighbour, I mean they're not exactly forthcoming you know, not exactly falling over themselves the people round here." "You poor thing," Anna Moreau said. "You must often be very very lonely." Eve said yes one did, yes at times one missed company and intelligent conversation and that. Meaning that they both did, that she and Adam both missed their friends and the city sometimes but that really it wasn't very, and Anna Moreau said that what Eve needed was to join the little Support Group for Women that she'd started. "It is informal you know, we drink a little coffee, we talk of our problems – the health, the children, contraception, *you* know. One feels so very less alone I think ... "

"Oh here's Adam coming!" Eve could have danced. "Let's hear what he thinks."

Adam came into the room smiling a welcome, carrying by some unfortunate chance a rolled-up copy of the extreme right-wing magazine he'd been consulting for his lecture. Anna Moreau's pale wide eyes fastened on it, grew paler and wider. Part of Eve stood aside watching her maliciously, but another small secret part was ashamed, cringingly ashamed of the paper as it had been ashamed earlier of the neat synthetic dress from Monoprix. Couldn't he have bloody well quoted from *Libération*? It's so unimportant, she hissed at herself, well OK, agreed, so we're making statements about ourselves but what we're stating ... what I'm stating is that I haven't time to, that I just don't notice what, and if my husband wants to quote from, well anyway who cares if Anna Moreau thinks we're unfrequentable, catch yourself on. "*Minute*, the magazine for tiny minds!" she joked uneasily. Anna Moreau said nothing and glanced away quickly.

"Oh Adam, Doctor Moreau's organising a little Human Rights festival, she wants to know if we'll help. All the professional people. To prove our solidarity with the Central American peasants. Real ethnic food and everything, she says."

"Yes but prove it to whom?" Adam asked politely. "Have you invited some generals? Someone from the CIA? Shall our lives be in any danger?"

"It is a gesture," Anna Moreau said stiffly. "One cannot merely stand by … " "One can, one can, one has to!" Adam exclaimed. "Tell me what else can one do? Remember the no-nuke demos? The Peace People? Chile and Afghanistan? Pollution of our lovely beaches? All those wasted Sundays standing up to be counted. Except that no one bothered to count us, did they? Except ourselves. We'd have been as well at Mass."

"Listen," Anna Moreau turned to Eve, "I think *you* were interested, no? I shall leave these pamphlets with you, they tell all about it, about what is happening there, the atrocities. I am sure that you will decide to join us, it is a very good cause."

Eve left her to the door. "I am returning, if I may, another time. A day when your husband works. And we shall discuss this terrible slaughter together, also my little Group for Women, yes?"

"Oh please do," Eve said politely. "Come any time, I'm nearly always here." The pale eyes softened, Anna Moreau took Eve's hand in a gentle nunlike grip: "How terribly terribly sad that sounds," she breathed.

Eve ran upstairs to the room where Adam was typing again. "She took you for a right old fascist, our Anna. Did you see her, couldn't tear her beady eyes off *Minute*, better burn it publicly on the village square when you're finished."

"Well bang goes any hope of a social life now, that's the last we're going to see of the local élite."

"How terribly terribly sad zat sounds! No but she'll be back, she wants to adopt me, thinks I'm down-trodden."

"Ah yes, but are you a professional person? Are any of us – is that our métier, would you say, being people?" Eve stopped laughing: "It's incredible though isn't it, making a carnival on the backs of – "

"Anyhow I can't say I'll pine much for the lovely Anna, couldn't really fancy her personally. Those little green legs!"

Eve felt, like a betrayal, the distance opening between their two understandings. "But that's hardly the point Adam, she didn't come here as a *woman* to be fancied or whatever, she came as a ghastly well-meaning human being, that's how we ought to be judging her."

"Oh Christ if you want to be *feminist* about it!"

Eve went slowly downstairs. Was this all it amounted to, this famous life of the intellect, this pair of supposedly united souls standing by their wide-open window looking for truth? Was that all, slogans and petty insults, and mediocrity itself perceived only as an unattractive woman in green tights?

"It's the price that lot has to pay for inventing Descartes," she joked silently, "condemned to spend their time classifying life and filing it away neatly in wee pigeonholes. A woman is female therefore logically … " Arming herself in rueful contempt against the bruising that, she supposed, was an inevitable result of leaving her rose-coloured room.

"How unimportant it all is," she told the baby, "How futile! Feminism and peppered bananas. And you, where are *you* going to end up in all this? You just going to drift from womb to grave like the rest of us, eh? Or are you going to be the one that comes blazing out of the flames like an avenging angel? You'd damn well better be, old son!"

She put him back in his cot, fetched her notebook from the landing cupboard, sat down by the open window and wrote, with a sort of stubborn despair: "Eve, in exile, sat aimlessly by a tall open window watching the sun slithering about on the slope of grass, the beech tree frozen helplessly into a posture, eternally awaiting some signal … "

Swan Song

It was the heart of a glorious summer but for once the young mother was unable to enjoy it. She was in a desperate state of anxiety.

"The first five came out perfect," she wept, "but would someone for the love of God come and tell me what's wrong with this one?"

The old neighbour had seen plenty of sights in her day but this big feathery lump with the long neck had her stumped. She would have liked to offer some comfort but in the circumstances there was little anyone could do except utter the vague pieties of optimism: "Ah it'll come out all right with the help of God. It looks healthy enough anyhow. Sure in a month or so you won't be able to tell the difference."

"The drake'll slaughter me," moaned the poor mother, "after all I went through, sitting on them eggs day in day out for weeks, it's not fair, how will I face him?"

"Don't be daft, missus!" the old duck said. "You have six fine healthy ducklings to show him, won't he be delighted with you!"

The drake was not delighted. "Do you take me for a right cod altogether? You hunkered down under some young turkey-cock or another when you got my back turned you huer you!" But even he had to admit that the thing bore no resemblance to a young turkey. Or to a goose or chicken or guinea-hen. And it could swim; it was a fine strong swimmer for its age.

"Some fault in your breed," he decided, "some old deformity or another in one of your ancestors. Shaming me!" he said, "shaming the life out of me!" He was an anxious waddling little creature who lived in constant dread of being shamed, defiantly proud of his family and his way of life but perpetually expecting both to be ridiculed, haunted as he was by an ingrained sense of inferiority to the tall strutting farmyard birds who were his neighbours.

But he was a decent enough drake for all that, pious and respected and anxious to do the best he could for his children. He tried to be fair to his ugly offspring, made great efforts not to favour the others more. It was difficult. Apart from eating and swimming, the thing seemed to have no natural duck instincts. She was awkward with her brothers and sisters, snapped and pecked when they were slow at catching her meaning. And she never right learned how to quack.

"She's a bit backward," the mother sighed, "I fear the poor creature will never be too right in herself!"

"She's an oddity," the drake announced openly in the yard, feeling he might somehow soften the disgrace if he came out with the news himself before the neighbours got a chance to. "A big awkward bawky of a thing! I'm afraid she's going to have a hard enough time of it when she gets out and about in the world. She'll be a laughing-stock, the smart ones'll all take a han' at her!"

The ugly duckling listened and watched and gradually became aware that she was a thing of little value. She clung nervously to her mother, dreading the day she'd have to venture out from the shelter of her wings, memories still clinging to her like bits of eggshell of a time when even she was enclosed and safe and intact.

When she was old enough to be let loose with the others in the yard of the farm she hung back timidly at first, imagining herself slashed and pecked at by a thousand foreign beaks, then broke away from her sisters in terror and hid herself under a leafy bush. She had the life scared out of her there by a big shambling red hen who peered beadily into her face, gave an amazed "Och-och-och-och!" and let go a squirt of caac straight under her bill. A deliberate insult, thought the ugly duckling. It's beginning, she thought, they weren't long starting to make a laughing-stock of me.

She stood her ground under the bush all day, afraid to move, longing for home but scared to venture out across the crowded space that separated her from the friendly familiar pond.

"Well how did you all get on?" the mother asked in the evening, already treating them as adults, already preoccupied by the new clutch of eggs she was hatching.

"We got on all right except for *her*," they chorused, "It seems Lady Muck here thinks she's too good for the rest of us. Would you believe it, Mammy, her ladyship stood preening herself under a bush all day and wouldn't talk to no-one! You should hear what they're all saying about her."

"I knew it," the father moaned, "I *said* she'd make a cod of herself. The big oddity, is she right in the head at all I wonder? If God hasn't said it she'll bring shame on the whole lot of us before she's finished!"

The ugly duckling listened. She wasn't right in the head. She wasn't right in the body either. Her understanding was slow. What place could there be for her among all these neat little chicks and ducklings with their bright eyes and gossipy cluckings, so sure and so confident of their place in the yard? *Her* place was to hide, to shrink against walls, to be invisible.

But they wouldn't let her. It became a habit that as soon as she showed herself in the yard they pounced on her in a mob, quacking and cackling and hissing and gobbling. They jostled and pushed her, asked quick cheeky questions and didn't wait to hear her slow reasoned replies. She had no gift at all for the smart answer; it was another great lack in her.

The torment never lasted long and as she grew older she learned to endure it silently. If she didn't attempt to explain herself to them they soon got bored and went off on their own occupations, just flinging a puff of cheeping giggles in her direction when they remembered to.

Standing ignored in a corner, she closely observed the life of the farmyard. Every single one of the creatures there belonged to a different breed from her. The hens scratched and scrabbed at the dust with anxious worried expressions as if they expected every worm they found to be their last, muttering neurotically under their breaths, raising their heads now and then to nod to a neighbour with a sighed "Och-och-och-och!" Shawled old turkeys paced through the yard with pious intolerant faces and large bodies weighed down with dignity. A cat snaked under the laurel hedge, hunted with quiet enjoyment, then lay yawning in the sun for hours, twitching the tip of his tail for amusement.

The first time the ducklings saw the tail twitch they leaped back with terrified excited quacks; the ugly duckling alone realised that the tail was not some creeping sinister thing but part of the animal called cat.

She quietly examined the tail, the fur, the independent lazy length of creature poured out under the sunny laurels, belonging to no litter, no clutch, no herd. Belonging, incredibly and magnificently, to himself.

Swan Song

Is it so bad to be different, she wondered, such a crime to be unlike? There's other things besides duck, she thought aloud, things flying in the air, things crawling along the ground, a being could be anything, be cat, be crow, be ...

Two chickens caught her muttering, lifted her off her feet with a screech: "She thinks she's a cat, thinks she's a cat! Cat cat cat!" Ran round the farmyard cackling insanely: "Thinks she's a cat! Thinks she's a cat!"

From that out, her nickname was Cat. Worse, it became her family's nickname. Any duckling or adult duck, even the most aged and pious of relatives, venturing too far from its pond heard the name indiscriminately hissed, barked, mooed, cackled, gobbled, grunted: Cat! Cat! Meeaw there, Cat!

Her brothers and sisters hated her for it, were ashamed of her, resented her existence. "You've made *us* a laughing stock now as well as yourself!" They considered themselves to be moving up in life, had all achieved a middling class of respectability, repaying the sacrifices their poor parents made to rear them. "You've made us the laughing stock of the whole world!"

"It's not the whole world," she said thoughtfully, awed with discovery, looking up at the sky, across the meadows, down to the bog with its strange high grasses, scummy bottomless pools, its secret alien voices. "If you think this narrow yard is the whole world!"

They flung themselves on her, pecked her cruelly, chased her from their presence. The drake, cringing under his family's shame, stabbed her with sharpened insults which frequently drove her into mad tempests of rage and protest. When that occurred he called her a poor wild class of a being, hysterical, a nervous wreck.

The mother had no comfort to offer, her mind now entirely filled with continuous hatching. Maybe if her daughter had been weaker, prettier, slighter-limbed ... Both duck and drake felt they could have loved and protected something small and ill-grown, something fluffy and sick, could have found a vocation in devoting whole lifetimes to making much of it, to saving it from hurt.

The ugly duckling was too big for that, too awkward with her great spagues of legs, her long snake's neck, the arrogant set of her head.

For her own sake they made efforts to teach her meekness, the drake roaring rage like thunder, the duck quacking sweet reason: "If you don't learn your place you'll have no sort of life, Daughter. You have to be good and modest and humble in this yard, conduct yourself like the ones around you, ask no questions, do all that we bid you, find a nice decent drake and hatch out your eggs when the time comes, be a credit to your parents in their old age."

"Why?" she asked, "What good will happen if I do all those things? What bad if I don't?"

"You belong to this yard, you belong to us," they said.

"Let you not forget how your poor mother sat hatching you for long weeks when she might have been out enjoying the summer like all the rest. How she looked after you when you were small, deprived herself of food to nourish you, spent her precious time teaching you everything she knew. All we ask in return is respect and obedience and a bit of ordinary common gratitude."

The duckling thought: but I never chose to belong to this yard, never asked to be hatched, what did she bother for? Then, aghast at the treason of such a thought, she made haste to bury it under quick agreement: "You are right. I owe you everything. I'll try to be good from this out."

Crucified with remorse for past badness she kept well away from the laurel hedge and the shameless independent cat. She followed her mother closely from place to place, pouring out affection in great foreign-sounding quacks. "Oh give my head peace!" the duck exclaimed at last, "I have more to do than drag a big lump of a daughter with me wherever I go. If you want to please me just do as you're bid and be like everyone else!"

The duckling could not be like everyone else but she wore herself out trying, walked humped up with her neck pulled in to make it shorter, painfully taught herself to utter civil meaningless quacks, stood on the edge of the farmyard observing avidly how the sophisticated featherheads walked, spoke, conducted themselves. "What's that bawky stuck there gaping at?" they chittered, "Meeaow! She must be watching a mousehole!"

She learned to stand in the dimmest corner behind the dunghill and peer out humbly, sidelong, from ashamed eyes. From time to time, the fattest young cockerel in the farmyard would leap on to the dunghill and sing out a song of praise to himself, of glory to the farmyard. The hens would stop scratching to listen entranced till he leaped down again, then scatter themselves before him in a cloud of delighted cackling giggles, pretending to flee but taking good care to stay well within his reach, submissive. She noticed her sisters fleeing in the same slavish way before the young drakes. Though she found the drakes squat and unattractive, and the whole performance humiliating, she knew it was her duty to do likewise, and spent hours practising the breathless giggling flight, the abject brokenbacked surrender.

Neither drake nor rooster made any move to jump on her, and she concluded that this, too, was something far beyond her talents. Shamefully she crept back to her place behind the dunghill.

Standing like that one day, she saw a Man approach, seize the magnificent young cockerel, wring his neck, and carry him by the legs to the kitchen door, his poor head gruesomely dangling.

She stood still in an instant of disbelief, then flew on stumbling wings to warn her parents, to warn the ducklings, hens, pigs, dogs of the obscene destiny that lay in wait for them. To tell them that *this* was what it was all for, *this* was the end of the good behaviour, the flocking and herding, scratching and scrabbing, the weeks of laborious hatching.

They said she was lying, said she wasn't right in the head, said: Look, the rooster's up there singing where he always sings!

She looked and saw that a younger, slightly thinner, cock had immediately taken the place of the first. The young pullets and old hens noticed no difference, listened fascinated to his song, then scattered with submissive cluckings before him.

She pointed out differences in his colour, his size, and everyone stared blankly at her till she trailed into silence.

They can't all be mistaken, she told herself, so it must be me. I *must* be away in the head. My brain is sick, my eyes not to be trusted, better keep quiet.

But somewhere deep in her mind she knew what she had seen, and the knowledge added a new level of hopelessness to the jeers and the peckings and the torment. To live patiently with all this, and for what? Some day a hand reaches out and ...

I must go away, she thought. I am in every way different from these creatures. My own parents are the first to admit it. I have arrived in this yard by some ridiculous accident, an egg dropped perhaps as someone flew over ...

But in that case, she thought, it is only logical to suppose that I arrived *from* somewhere, that there exists a place where a being like me is normal. She thought with wonder of a distant world where she need never be

Swan Song

mocked or lonely, where every day flocks of creatures like herself fearlessly stretched their long necks towards the sun, opened their great wings to rise above dust and dunghill and narrow farmyard pond. A world where one could live for whole centuries without fear of the hen's beak, or the dog's bark, or the wrung neck.

"I'm going away," she told her mother. "You have been very good to me and I shall always be grateful, but I have to go away now and search for my own kind."

"*Away*?" the mother asked, "*Where* away?" she cried, "You're breaking my heart with your foolishness, Daughter, there *is* no away. This is your home, this yard is the place you belong to. This yard, this pond, what else is there? There's nowhere to go, child, it's all just your wild imaginings!"

"The meadows, the lake, the marsh," the duckling stumbled, "My own people ... "

The drake puffed out his feathers, poised himself for attack: "From the first day she came out of that egg her ladyship's done nothing only despise us and make little of us. A poor nervous oddity that even the rats and mice make a fool of! The meadows, the lake, the marsh!" he mimicked, "Big jawbreakers of words from God knows where! Can't she even lower herself to talk like the rest of us?"

Every word was accompanied by a blow: blow of wing, of strong webbed feet, of flat hard bill. The five other ducklings joined delightedly in the attack. The mother duck stood aside, weeping silently, making no attempt to interfere. Her heart was broken, this was all she'd ever expected. From the very nest she'd been taught that a mother's lot is a hard one, that from the minute you laid your first egg you need expect neither peace nor enjoyment, nor the slightest pick of gratitude from them you hatched.

The ugly duckling's feathers flew in all directions, a wing was broken, an eye damaged. The chickens danced around mockingly, the dogs barked ferociously, the old turkeys muttered scandalised prayers. The cat under the laurels yawned and thought it served the poor fool right: if she'd had the gumption to leave them all behind long ago and follow the example he gave her ...

"Your own people!" the drake jeered, "And who might they be when they're at home, eh?" He jerked a sarcastic wing towards the sky and turned with a laugh to the gaping delighted audience: "Maybe she thinks them's her own people, them big-shots up yonder! Well go on then, miss, go on, there's none of *us* holding you back! Fly up to them if you're fit. Let us all see what sort of a welcome the high-ups'll give you!"

The ducklings and chickens let out a whooping guldher of a cheer as three magnificent swans shaded the yard for a moment with their great stormy wings. The ugly duckling didn't even bother to look up: she used the distraction to escape and limp away ungainly and bleeding to her corner behind the dunghill.

None of the swans looked down as they flew over the little farmyard. They never did look down. They knew there was never anything worth looking down at.

Mixed Marriage

"Now that's all very well," she protested, "but it'd only need someone a bit colour-blind up there and *I'd* soon find myself repatriated to Algiers!" Even when she'd realised they were *not* joking (were, incredibly, *not* doing a send-up of the racist clichés you kept seeing these days in cheap newspapers), Alice had managed to restrain herself from leaping with a snarl and a growl to the defence of minority groups, immigrant workers and the ex-colonised. Instead, she'd reminded herself once again (though admittedly with rather more irritation this time) that Leon's elder brother and sister had not been lucky enough to have all his advantages, that they'd been born too soon to profit as he had done from the revolutionary liberalism of the sixties and seventies, that they were simply two nice decent lyonnais shopkeepers married to two other nice decent etcetera and that for Leon's sake, for courtesy's sake, for the space of one short weekend.

So: "That's all very well," she protested as humorously as she could, "but it'd only need … " They looked at her out of large kind sensible faces, quite unstartled, quite unshaken. Hidebound, she thought (not without admiration), solidly bound in good quality French hide.

You could read your way, she thought, from Aragon to Zola, dropping in on Céline and Courteline, Daudet and Flaubert and Mauriac and Maupassant and there they'd be, the backbone of their country, one or two of them for ballast on every page, clichés of themselves. Caricatures of La France Profonde. It was one of the things she found hardest to take, the way even the nicest of them turned out to be in the end great big humourless caricatures of themselves. Huguette and Marcelle beef to the heels in well-cut drip-dry dresses suitable to their age, weight, and social level; the brother and the beau-frère the worthiest of citizens, their neat round bellies and massive backsides bearing ample witness to over fifty years of meals like the one that was now roasting, boiling, simmering, chilling, freezing, thawing, maturing, achieving room temperature in the gadget-filled fake rustic kitchen of their *résidence secondaire typique*.

She pictured millions of foreign tourists piously pursuing The Real France in gîtes ruraux, relais routiers, cathedrals, brothels, chateaux on the Loire, crêpes suzettes, son et lumière, feeds of snails and going home (home satisfied, mark you!) never knowing they'd missed reality by a mile. Throw open my in-laws to the public, she thought, roll up! roll up! Five francs a time to join us here on the terrace of their restored farmhouse, *that* is the authentic folklore.

Such small internal revolts were succeeding in getting her smoothly through the weekend. Had been succeeding up till now. And really not such revolts as all that. Because one of the things she'd always found *easiest* to take, even away back in the days of the greasy-eyed, tediously-ritual Latin pass from every adolescent/père de famille/old age pensioner who gave her a lift (well, *especially* back then), had been precisely the touching way they always did turn out to be great big solemn caricatures of themselves. They were easy to take. If you wanted to take them. As of course Alice did. Had been doing for a good many years now, in the accepted Biblical manner: your country is my country, your people are my people. But diluted, she thought, remembering gratefully that Paris and the cosmopolitan daily life to which she would return tomorrow evening were (and in spite of the reconciliation would continue to be) nine hundred lovely kilometres north of this particular aspect of La France Profonde. Remembering too their own *résidence secondaire* in Spain which (reconciliation or no reconciliation) would continue to prevent them spending any but the most once-in-a-blue-moon weekend in the bosom of these nice ordinary decent ...

Leon, in the nice ordinary decent bosom of his family, looked like a changeling, and thank God for that, but of course he *was* twelve or thirteen years younger. What might he have been like if ... ? (What would he be like when ... ?) But Leon, naturally, would never be like that, because being "like that" was as much a state of mind as the result of over-eating, over-drinking, over-possessing. You became "like that" from years and years of uttering, actually having the gall to utter, utter in the last quarter of the twentieth century, utter in *public*, without blushes or doubts or hesitations, the extraordinary (no, all too ordinary, she feared) statements that for the past ten minutes her brothers-in-law and sisters-in-law had been calmly utt ... No, but do I want to take them, she wondered, do I *have* to take them?

These particular ones? Knowing that of course she had to and that, in very small doses, she was not really unhappy doing so.

Because in spite of everything she was enchanted to be there, to actually have a stake in a village that she'd always remembered with delight, that had struck her as little less than paradise when she'd come on it quite by accident that summer fifteen years earlier. How good it was after all that his father's death and this shared inheritance of house and land had reconciled Leon with his family and made it possible for them to be here sitting on the patio under the acacia tree resting their legs after the mad, but entirely charming, bustle of the market at Pont St Esprit, sipping their apéritif and whetting their appetites for yet another of Marcelle's lovely meals that would be rich in garlic and herbs and olive oil and talk. And talk.

Up to now the talk had been of a kind she wouldn't have listened to for five minutes in Paris or Ireland or anywhere else. In the twelve years Leon had been cut off from his family most of them seemed either to have died or to have developed the most unappetising disorders in the most embarrassing places, (and *how* they wallowed in all the details!) but here, she had to admit, such talk seemed right and suitable and (once you adjusted your mind to the tedium) even amusing in a bizarre way. Because she'd married Leon in the middle of the last devastating tribal row she'd met few of her in-laws. Those she had met were as dully prosperous and as dully nice as Charles and Marcelle and their spouses but the ones she hadn't met seemed to exist, delightfully, in a thick Rabelasian mist of rural folklore. Earlier when they were chopping *lardons* for the chicken, Marcelle had been reminded of l'oncle Raoul who always kept a large piece of fat bacon hanging beside the kitchen stove to rub on his piles, and all five of them had fallen about shrieking, recalling the story of his new daughter-in-law who hadn't been told and who, on her first Sunday there, had naturally chopped it up and cooked it in the *coq au vin*.

"Hou la la! Hou la la! La tête de la pauvre belle-mère!"

And, to her amazement, even scholarly civilised Leon had fallen about slapping his thighs and shrieking: "Merde alors! Ah bah me-e-erde alors, elle est bien bonne celle-là!"

Mixed Marriage

No, you had to come to the Midi for anecdotes like that, Alice had thought, basking in the exoticism of it all, downing her pastis and nibbling her olives and listening to her husband and in-laws being Latin for her delight. Basking in the lovely Midi that was welcoming her back: the smell of thyme, the lizards on the garden wall, grasshoppers going mad in the long grass beside the old *lavoir*, and the wild incessant music that drifted down the terraces of uncultivated vines. It was the music that had spoiled everything.

"Listen to them, just listen to them!" Marcelle had spat with startling venom, cutting across the brother's description of la pauvre Tante Jeannette's funeral. "Every weekend it's the same, polluting us with their disgusting Arab music!"

At that point Leon had hastily opened *Midi-Libre* and buried himself in the local news, leaving her to cope, appalled, with his family's quite appalling views on their Algerian neighbours. On all Algerians. On blacks. On immigrant workers in general.

"If we'd had the sense to elect Le Pen he'd have rid the country of them, sent them all back to the shanties they came out of. I've seen North Africa, I've seen them at home, barefoot, running barefoot half of them; how could savages like that fit in, in a country like France?"
"Repatriation!" the brother cried, "That's what you need. Clean up the country. A decent government up in Paris and ... "

"Now that's all very well," Alice protested at last, trying to be humorous about it, trying not to see the ill-bred soap box that was edging itself tactlessly up to her, nudging her to for godsake, for humanity's sake, get up on it at once and roar ... For after all they were Leon's family and they were nice ordinary decent people and she was their guest, bound by courtesy. "But it'd only need someone a bit colour-blind up there and *I'd* soon find myself repatriated to Algiers!"

"Oh we don't mean you, Alice," the brother was indulgent and everyone was smiling at her except Leon, screened behind *Midi-Libre*, "You are sympathique, Alice, you are civilised. We are aware of course that Ireland, (la belle Irlande si verte, si souriante!), well let us say she is not the most evolved of ... Enfin, she is not La France! But you are not savages, voyons! You *are* white, after all ... "

And the soap-box was there and she was stepping on it because you couldn't, with the best will in the world you couldn't let that pass without comment. Courtesy or no courtesy, as an Irishwoman (let's face it, from a country where the dirty likes of Uncle Raoul would be decently shut up in a home or someplace) you had to leap to the attack even if it meant deliberately crashing through the good-natured Saturday morning mood and mortally wounding these nice ordinary decent ...

"Oh being white is no guarantee," she snapped. "No guarantee one won't be betrayed. Not in France. The French Jews were white, weren't they, and nobody lifted a finger to save them. *Au contraire*," she accused bitterly. But amazingly none of the four showed the slightest sign of being wounded; the statement that had seemed so outrageous, so demolishing in its implications for them that it shocked her own sensibilities to make it, aroused no painful emotions in them. They had no consciousness at all of their country's responsibility or their own for what had been done (or not done, she supposed) in their lifetime. It was another of the things she as an Ulster woman found hard to take: their complete lack of talent for assuming the weight of their own past. "Oh the Jews," the beauf said vaguely, "nobody's against the Jews nowadays you know. Those people have suffered enough. It was a long time ago."

"It was in *your lifetime*," she insisted.

"We were only children," Marcelle said. "But do you remember, Charles, when they came for that family what was their name two doors down, we were still living in Paris then ... Monsieur, monsieur what's this, he had a shop in the same street as Papa, it was the police came, not the Gestapo, just our own police so of course nobody thought ... We were all watching from the windows, we wouldn't have dared watch if the Germans had been there ... "

"And did nobody protest?" Alice asked fiercely. "Did you all just stand there behind the curtains and just let them be dragged away? Did nobody in that whole street *do* anything?"

"What did you expect them to do?" Leon snapped suddenly from behind his newspaper. "Rattle dustbin lids? We're talking about the Nazis for God's sake, not the British army in Belfast!"

"It was a very long time ago," the brother was placating, "Everyone thought they were just taking them to a camp."

"So they were," she said, "So they were! That's exactly where they took them, to a camp." Not daring to ask if the family had ever returned, not wanting to know.

"Pay no attention to Alice," Leon said, still behind the local paper, "My wife belongs to the generation that thought it could halt Armageddon by smoking pot and calling policemen pigs."

Not such a changeling after all, she thought, oh indeed no, doing his level best my little Leon to adapt. Small obedient brother, she thought, still trotting helplessly behind these big sensible siblings of his. Uneasily she recalled the ridiculous little incident of the evening before. "*Le Testament de Dieu,* Leon!" Marcelle had exclaimed, picking a paperback off the top of their luggage. "Don't tell me you're a practising Catholic again!"

"It's my wife's," said Leon, "Alice has decided to study

philosophy." Not in his normal voice but in such a uxoriously-indulgent tone that she immediately saw poor Bernard-Henri Levy dangling woolily off a pair of Pingouin knitting needles, a master of the decade's thought shrunken to the harmless pastime of a bored housewife.

"Hou la la! Philosophy!" Huguette had repeated, "And how does Alice find time to read books with a husband and two kids to look after? The washing, the cooking, the housework, not to mention your little teaching job, Alice, it can't leave you much time for philosophy!"

"Well, Leon does his half of the chores naturally," she'd begun without thinking and then stopped in confusion, confronted with the brother's and the beauf's expression of ribald astonishment and Leon's own momentary glance of hate, realising that she'd committed an act of public castration, demolishing her husband's masculinity in the eyes of his family, probably destroying any hopes he had of being accepted by them as an adult Latin male. Apparently he had not forgiven her ...

The patio was claustrophobic in the sunless humidity of late Spring. Gobbets of wet acacia blossom kept plopping down among the plates of olives.

"You've brought your Irish weather with you," Marcelle smiled and Huguette echoed: "Irish weather! Hou la la!" Great zinc-coloured clouds moved across the sky behind the top terrace where the Algerian couple and their teenage sons were camping beside their half-built bungalow. A high thin whinge of music had been drifting down steadily since early morning along with the chatter of birds and the scent of wild thyme.

"Listen to them! Just listen to them! Savages!" And it *was* annoying; enlightened or not you had to admit it was irritating, the whine of foreign music drifting down from the terraced heights where years ago there was only an old barn half-hidden in almond trees. Not perhaps that it *was* necessarily Algerian music, she thought, realising for the first time, with a small shock, that it sounded more like Madonna or one of those rather than the veiled Laila or Jasmine she'd been picturing up till then. And why had she been picturing, why after all assume, wasn't she as great a bitch as anyone assuming they'd be (they who were born here, who'd never even *seen* Algeria) listening to native folksongs? She smiled at the incongruous thought of her own two ever listening to the McPeake Family. Of herself ever. So it might well be Madonna or Patricia Kaas, one of those names you saw in *Time* or heard the children going on about. And how sad, she thought, not to know, how incredibly sad to have lost touch, to have so absentmindedly floated into middle-age. (My mother, she thought, my mother long ago who couldn't tell Bob Dylan from Elvis.) Her eyes filled with anise-flavoured tears, her throat had a real lump in it (a great deal of pastis had been drunk rather quickly in the last half-hour.) To think that even Dylan, and Neil Young and Joan Baez, those cool clear seekers of wisdom and truth, were receding back and back into that stout elderly drip-dry limbo of Acker Bilk and Bing Crosby and the Andrews Sisters and Maurice Chevalier and Gracie Fields and …

"I didn't vote for Le Pen myself," the brother was saying ("Vote for Le Pen!" Huguette giggled), "because I think *au fond* he is a little crazy. I cannot myself see him at the head of a great nation, but I'm with him all the way when it comes to the *bicots*, he knows what's what with the *bicots*, he knows what the sods are capable of. He was out there wasn't he, *he* did his Algerian war all right, he saw them murdering their masters!"

"Out there torturing," Alice muttered, but nobody was listening only Huguette. "Bloody para! It's a well-known fact that he tortured, the papers were full of it."

"Hou la la! Alice reads *Libération*!" Huguette said. "C'est la grande mode, la torture! Nothing else on the télé, Amnesty International, UNICEF, Project this and Project that, they smash our ears with torture nowadays. It's only a fashion."

"Like the Kurds and the Ethiopians," Marcelle agreed, "Mais qu'est ce qu'on déguste avec l'Ethiopie! As if we hadn't our own people to feed, our own unemployed."

"And who's responsible, you tell me that, Alice! Whose fault is it our youngsters can't find jobs, eh?"

"Well it's not mine," she laughed, to lighten the atmosphere. "Can't really see the Berlitz taking on three million unemployed Frogs to teach English, even if Le Pen did ship me out on the next plane! No thanks Marcelle, I won't have another. I think I'll just ... "

She thought of strolling up through the abandoned vines, past the line of apricot trees run wild, to stand on the highest terrace and look at the land falling away dramatically beneath her feet, the Rhône valley stretching for miles and miles with its well-behaved farms, its fat vineyards, dark columns of cypress trees, red-roofed houses with walls the colour of ripe melons. A landscape where the horizon didn't come down at the top of the next field. Paradise. But the grass would be high and wet alongside the vines, she had only her sandals, there would certainly be serpents. The vines had not been worked since long before her father-in-law's death; the old Italian immigrant who ran the place for him died several years earlier and it had been impossible to replace him or even to find farm labourers. The young local men had fled the land long ago and were earning good money in the big nuclear plant at Pierrelatte. (If she turned on her chair she could see the two stout waisted chimneys with soiled white blobs of smoke poised on top like button mushrooms on squat stalks.)

She recalled her fruit-picking days without any

particular nostalgia, without any particular sadness for the banal elderly couple of retired shopkeepers who'd employed her and later, reluctantly, become her parents-in-law. What she did remember with delight was the high ridge at the head of the vines where the land jumped unexpectedly from under your feet and scampered away laughing towards an endless blue horizon. When you grew up in Cross and the sky wedged down shut like a lid at the back of Bob's hill, McCreesh's field, the Long Loanin and the Pigeonhouse Rock (shutting you in with your past and your prejudices, your narrow little alliances and hatreds and fears) you dreamed of a place where the horizons were limitless, where the winds blew in freely from everywhere carrying a thousand scents and a thousand songs. But, as they said, the weather was untypical and the vines unwalkable in.

"The stink of their spices in the market this morning," Huguette was complaining, "Like a souk. They've managed to turn Pont into a souk. And all those women in veils, on n'est plus chez soi! If they must live here the least they could do is blend in a bit." She smoothed a fold of houndstooth polyester over her plump knees.

"Four wives each!" the beauf exclaimed primly, a domesticated orgy twinkling away in the liquid shallows of his eyes, "And every one of them drawing child allowance. Who pays for it, want me to tell you the mugs that's paying for all that?"

The brother turned excitedly to Alice: "We've applied for revolver permits, you know. Stands to reason. I said to the gendarmes I said they've got three big sons up there and who knows how many uncles and cousins and ... It's not myself I'm thinking of but what's the point of being a man is what I say if you're not prepared to stand up and protect your womenfolk?"

He breathed pastis heavily over her: "Even seen one of

their knives? Even seen an Algerian knife have you?"

His little brown eyes gleamed in the grey sweating expanse of his face and for an instant she found herself trapped in the unreasoning terror she saw there: commando knives, Muslim fanatics, the insult of a French throat swiftly slit in the night, veins emptying themselves rippling and gurgling over the quarry tiles. For that instant she was with them, one of them, inescapably married into their dark tribal fears, her heart pounding yes yes it could happen, it *was* possible you heard stories terrible stories ...

But his voice was abruptly switched off by a group of jet fighters screaming in low formation beneath the clouds, ripping hysterically through the grey metal fabric of the sky, and she was able to rescue her eyes and breathe. She lip-read: "From the training base at Orange, they'll be back and forth all day."

By the time they'd gone she was able to say calmly: "But I've been in France all these years and never once have I heard of anyone having his throat cut by an immigrant worker! God it would have been all over the papers, the télé would have gone mad! It's just stories."

"You can't trust them," the brother said. "Ever look at their faces did you, ever see their expressions? Repatriation's too good for them. If it was me," he continued, tapping her urgently on the knee, "do you know what I'd do? I'd pack the lot of them on to a ship with a ton of explosives and I'd send it out into the middle of the Mediterranean and I'd blow it up, that's what I'd do!"

She looked to Leon for support but he was apparently fascinated by the local football results, refusing to become involved. For the first time she realised that storming out of his parents' home to marry her had been the only act of rebellion in his whole life. At the moment she found this more disquieting than flattering.

She wondered what was the sanest way of dealing with

the brother's extraordinary outburst. Just fall about laughing? Or try to give it, and him, dignity with a serious reply? Because after all mightn't this be their way of assuming the weight of their past? Mightn't it be possible to interpret his remarks as an unadmitted admission of racial guilt, a sublimated awareness of the sheer logic, the inevitability, the rightness of eventually having one's throat cut by the people one had battened on for over a century? But no, don't be daft, she told herself, that's a very Irish interpretation: the logic of the colonised, not of the ex-colonist. It would be silly and pretentious of her to try and impose dignity and deep meanings on what was no more, probably, than a peevish letting-off of steam by a hardworking man who couldn't even enjoy his weekend cottage in peace.

She thought again gratefully of their own cottage high up above red arid fields: leathery old men driving their few sheep along a village street enveloped in a thick everlasting smell of lanolin, a small crowded chapel crammed with bleeding images, old toothless welcoming women preparing chick-peas on smiling doorsteps. In a few weeks they'd be there, spending the summer as they spent every summer: accepted, innocent, free. Reinventing the simplicity of an imaginary impossible childhood. (Well aware that in cities down the dizzy hairpin roads the real children of the village were belatedly kicking their way into the squalor of the century, returning, if at all, for a disdainful yearly visit.) Families *are* for once a year, she thought, my own back at home or this lot, it's all one. Once you accepted that, they were easy enough to take. Not monsters, not to be fought; *they* had neither battened nor betrayed, they had fired no shots and planted no bombs. They're innocent bystanders like ourselves, she thought, as guilty and as helpless as bystanders always are. Imagine, she thought, the poor brother charging up that hill there with a loaded revolver, he'd *die*! Wouldn't he melt! It's all talk, that's all it is, she reassured herself. Talk.

She smiled across at Marcelle, making amends: "I'll never forget the first time I came here. It was the middle of the night and this lorry dropped us off at a crossroads near Pierrelatte, me and the friend I was hitching with. Anyhow there was a bit of waste ground full of thyme and stuff, I'll never forget the smell of that in the dark, and we didn't even bother opening the tent, we were flat out so we just spread our sleeping-bags on the thyme. It was like a mattress, all springy. And then about an hour later we woke up all crusted over with snails. They were everywhere, all over us, our eyelids, lips, everywhere, tiny little dry snails. Like babes in the wood we were. So we climbed back unto the road and sat there smelling the thyme and picking snails out of our hair, waiting for the dawn."

She did not add that when dawn came what they saw straight in front of them was the double electrified fence, the two stout waisted chimneys vomiting slow smoke, an ugly estate of factory workers' bungalows with synthetic red roofs, and the makeshift huddle of immigrants' shacks. It would have spoiled the story. One was always happier asleep with the cliché image: snails, thyme, cigales among the vines. Chick-peas and the smell of sheep. Spices on a market stall.

"Fantastic experience," she added, "It seemed the very essence of La Belle Fra – " Her voice was abruptly silenced as the brother's had been, as the grasshoppers, the birds, the simmering chicken, the Algerians' music, were all silenced by another group of fighter jets whose presence momentarily flattened the lovely landscape to nonentity, whose speed pulled the limitless horizons up close like defensive barricades, whose busy aggressive scream lulled even Alice with the comforting lying promise that almighty power was there, ready and arrogant, ultimately capable of protecting La Belle France against any danger that might menace her.

Then the meal was ready, and they all trooped in happily to eat it.

The Prize

Palermo was the making of him, Ireland helped, the disappearance of his mother and his four wives was no inconsiderable blessing, but what finally set Jonathan dancing happily down the road to fame was a sour little magazine article entitled 'The Disease of the Irish Cottage Industry'. It was not so much that the piece had any great literary or critical value – he wondered indeed what personal failure at lace work or Aran knitting led the author to take such a heavy hammer to such a graceful butterfly – but it did contain some very valuable information. All over Ireland, it seemed, perfectly virile men were discovering that the needle is lighter than the spade and were busy turning out more or less professionally adequate works of art in wool, silk, hemp, and scraps of discarded material. An accumulated weight of solitude, self-contempt and furtive guilt was lifted off Jonathan's shoulders: the article in the paper had put the nihil obstat on his life's work. He came out of the closet, quick.

Jonathan himself was only remotely Irish. On his father's side he was descended from a prominent Sicilian family that for centuries had roamed and robbed on land and sea, leaving by-blows in every port and racketeering gangs in every suburb. His mother was a third-generation Liverpool dressmaker who, on her lover's disappearance, set about earning a respectable living and bringing her son up decently in the fear of God, sex, beauty and good food. Not, however, the most perceptive of women, she saw no harm at all in letting wee Jonathan stand by her side for hours in their freezing attic room, his teeth chattering in time to the harsh music of the sewing-machine, his baby hands forming patterns with scraps of material and ends of coloured thread. Isn't he bright for his age, she said, and called the neighbours in to exclaim at the clever pictures he made. They exclaimed even more when he was fourteen and preferred to sit in the kitchen embroidering tray cloths while his little schoolmates were out chatting up birds and smashing up telephone kiosks.

His mother prayed for guidance, then took him aside to lecture him on the commoner forms of perversion, warn him against developing unmanly interests, and allude discreetly to the sacrifices she was making to rear him and the undying consideration she expected in return. Jonathan flung his arms about her neck, burst into tears, and vowed to be henceforth a faithful obedient son. Horrified at this further display of effeminacy she put him on the boat and sent him off to his great-uncle's farm in Ireland to be made a man of.

When he returned he was as manly as anyone could wish: six foot two with the face and build of a Mafia film star, a great appetite for the drink and the dogs, a healthy contempt for women, and a determination to do exactly as he pleased for the rest of his life. At seventeen he noticed that the man collecting protection money in the local betting shop was a dead ringer for himself, made exhaustive enquiries and then, with the family talent for persuasion, coaxed his father, if not to recognise him, at least to pay his way through art school.

His mother, whose livelihood was being seriously jeopardised by the increasing popularity of cheap off-the-peg fashion, was glad to have that much responsibility taken off her hands and surprisingly made no objection to the art school. (Her best friend's son was playing the guitar in a Hamburg cellar at that time and another neighbour's boy was doing very well indeed writing satire for the BBC.) She warned him about the temptations he might encounter, reminded him again of the sacrifices she'd made to bring him up single-handed, and expressed a wish that he might become a successful textile designer with a chain of boutiques and build her a villa with a swimming-pool.

He might well have done just that had he not, on graduating, been invited to spend the summer in his father's Renaissance palace in Sicily. Jonathan discovered beauty. He had never before seen so many paintings all together – it was as if half the National Gallery, Louvre and Prado were all rolled into one in his dad's collection. (This was indeed so: Don Battista acquired his pictures through a team of sharp-faced little men operating from basement offices in alleyways off the Rue de Rivoli, Trafalgar Square and Calle Cervantes.) But it was the tapestries that went to Jonathan's head. *There* was Art! No more messing about with brushes and turpentine, getting your hands filthy with charcoal, mixing and rubbing and cleaning and scraping like a Wimpy-bar cook. Just to sit at leisure by an open window thinking and dreaming and, stitch by perfect stitch, to construct a Universe. Jonathan had found his vocation.

He asked his father for money, a lot of money, and travelled East, West, North and South for inspiration. He was away five years and would have stayed longer but for the unfortunate liquidation of his father by the head of a rival family and the inevitable passing of his fortune to his legitimate offspring. As it was, Jonathan arrived back too late to, and indeed with no desire to, become part of the swinging creative British scene. With his mother's inherited peasant wisdom he had not spent all his money in the one shop and, after a few shrewd investments, he had enough left to buy the old homestead in Ireland where he had spent that dreary holiday as a boy.

He bought whitewash, bellows-wheels, and a ton of rushes and with his own hands stripped off the Celestial Blue gloss paint, the green synthetic roofing and the Howth stone facings. He tore out the furnace and radiators and donated them to the local church – buying, he hoped, years of clerical tolerance. Then he scoured Ireland hoping to find some crumbling ruin of a centenarian thatcher to add a bit of authenticity to the place. They were all dead long since but he came on a young American student who'd dropped out of college to learn the craft of his ancestors, and employed him.

During his search for a thatcher he'd happened to stop for a drink in the bar of a tourist hotel and had there discovered Sex, in the person of an expensive King's Road beauty over for the Horse Show. Aware that even the gift of an oil-fired central heating system wasn't going to buy him that much priestly tolerance, he felt obliged to marry her.

Immediately after the wedding Cynthia insisted that they return to London and, once there, forced him to look for a job in advertising. With his Liverpool accent he had no problem finding one and the cottage, reduced to the condition of a nineteenth-century hovel at a cost of half a million, became their holiday hideout. Even there he was unable to start producing the masterpieces that were burning holes in his soul: Cynthia made him take up manly hobbies like golf and tennis and told him if he wanted to be creative he could do something about the overgrown garden in front of the house; it was dragging down the value of the property, she said.

In the end his childhood habit of obedience was the making of him: he did as he was bid, cleared away the briars, dug over the ground and, in a flash of inspiration, buried Cynthia under it – sitting down that same evening to fill a canvas with the harmony of lustrously-gleaming blues and golds that, many years later, was to cause six of his half-brothers to massacre one another in public in a fit of acquisitive jealousy. He called it 'New Life' and sent it to a gallery in Paris whose owner, a lovely young eccentric of noble birth, enthusiastically invited him to send her as much work as he could produce. He planted pedigree roses over Cynthia, told the sympathetic neighbours that she couldn't stand rural life and, after the proper interval, divorced her for desertion.

Hardly had he settled down to the bliss of creative freedom than his mother, abandoning her Liverpool attic, arrived to take care of him. She took one dismayed look at her big hulk of a son sitting sewing all day and wallowing in snails, gazpacho and Jacques Brel records every evening and she went on her knees for guidance. Was he not ashamed of himself after all the sacrifices she made and the good decent bringing-up she gave him, there was never none of that in her family, and say what you like about his poor daddy it was the last thing anyone could accuse him of, and so *that's* why his unfortunate wife left him, the disgrace of it, and she could never hold up her head again the longest day she lived and would he not for her sake, the sake of a hardworking Irish mother, go out and look for a good decent job ... Poor Jonathan wept and flung his arms around her neck as he had done at fourteen, only this time he didn't let go. She went to keep Cynthia company under the roses and he sat down to begin another canvas.

But something had changed. The infallibility of the Irish mother (though diluted, in Jon's case, by three generation's exile and a lively hood for a father) is a doctrine which has

The Prize

caused many a good man to set his feet piously on the road to mediocrity. Jonathan took up golf again, found a job on a marketing magazine in Dublin, and spent much of his spare time trying to prove his virility – luckily a difficult task in Holy Ireland and one leading to much frustration which our hero, like many a better bachelor, converted into a sort of spiritual rabies. His tapestries, done now secretly on his odd free evenings, became bitter little allegories of the human condition. The gallery owner, aware that she had a genius on her hands, flew over to see him and, seeing him, set about marrying him. Ecology being in fashion then she taught him to rear silkworms and dye his own thread with roots, lichen, and boiled-up onion skins. The marriage was, however, a mistake. With sexual fulfilment the soul had gone out of his work and Marie-Claude, with her race's simpleminded devotion to Culture, volunteered to sacrifice herself and join her mother-in-law and Cynthia in the garden. He took over the gallery in Paris and continued to produce and sell work in his wife's name. Though in practice completely free he still felt his wild creative spirit somewhat hampered by being, legally, a married man and divorced her, like Cynthia, for desertion.

The divorce was as much a mistake as the marriage that led up to it since it left no obstacle at all in the path of big Doris Muldoon who'd fancied him ever since he joined the magazine and who now took advantage of his grief (genuine: he'd liked Marie-Claude) to march him once more to the altar. When, accustomed to his previous wife's enthusiasm for his Art, he showed Doris the canvas on which he was working she burst into a cackle of Convent-reared giggles and rushed off to ring her friends and the editor ...

Poor Johnny, the neighbours said, he had an awful talent for picking flighty ones and, seeing him garden so energetically to bury his sorrow, they offered him rose-slips and begonia cuttings as tokens of comfort. Doris had been a Catholic and it took ten years and many thousands of pounds to obtain an annulment. Happily, before he was quite bankrupt, an obliging Interpol agent happened to spot a woman who closely resembled her, vowed to silence in a Bangkok monastery, and he was free again.

When the marketing magazine closed down he continued anonymously to put his vision of the world on canvas and to live, unhindered, with the mixture of sensual indulgence and ascetic puritanism that was his legacy from his dead parents. It was then that he read the bit in the paper and was able to welcome, openly, the announcement that Bounderbury Chocolates (Ireland) Limited were offering three prizes of a thousand pounds each for the most original pieces of creative needlework in any medium, to be chosen by a panel of distinguished judges from, the sponsors hoped, a nationwide entry.

He submitted a canvas on which he had already been working enthusiastically for several months – a bleak terrifying cameo in green silk, each skein hand-dyed to the exact nuance he required. Olive-green of armies, sly poison green, green of ivy strangling broken cities, of mildew in deserted houses, of moss creeping over untended graves; green of dead tropical birds, of undisturbed Arctic ice, all merging into a background of green resurrected grass – plains and steppes, pampas and savannahs – stretching emptily away in a vast desolation of loneliness. The loneliness of a God who had rejected Man. He called it *Aftermath*. Then, feeling that there was no need to scatter clues around like Agatha Christie, he sent it off to Bounderbury House entitled simply 'Green'.

It won a prize (he had been aware that it might), was with the others well spoken of by the judges who claimed to be deeply impressed by the high standard of imagination and craftsmanship shown by all the entrants –

The Prize

a surprisingly high number for a first competition – and hoped to meet the three laureates at a reception to be held in Bounderbury House later that month. All very gratifying, but Jonathan felt a slight chill on hearing the further remarks of two of the judges interviewed on the bilingual Culture Anocht programme. What a pity, commented the editor of 'Craft Today', that unlike the good ladies of Bayeux he had not thought it necessary to sing the sorrows of his native land on canvas. And how odd, added the distinguished Catholic painter, that all three winners – indeed every one of the ninety thousand entrants – saw fit to ignore the sexual revolution that for some decades now had been laying its horny hand on our whores eh shores.

He wrote letters to both ladies, assuring the first that if she wanted the Battle of the Boyne in coloured thread any souvenir shop from Portrush to the Shankill Road would be only too glad to oblige, and begging the second to lead him (quickly quickly, he was starving!) towards this orgy of sexuality that she alone appeared to have discovered. As far as he could see the aims and ambitions of Irish girlhood had hardly changed since his first visit to a dancehall as a prurient teenage tourist thirty years before. How often, between marriages, had he trailed home from parties with his tail between his legs or, as poor Jacques so cunningly put it, 'la bite sous le bras', reflecting bitterly that the only effect of the permissive society on rural and urban Ireland was that now they expected you to buy them Pernod instead of an orange mineral before they kicked you in the teeth in the back seat. He didn't post either letter, feeling that he could discuss both points more effectively when he met the judges at the winners' reception.

Because all three prizewinners were men (storming, as the *'Emancipated Irishman'* had it, the last portcullis in what was traditionally a female stronghold) the competition results were given wide coverage in the national press as well as in the more specialised arts and crafts weeklies. Enthusiastic young reporters knocked on his door. Cosmopolitan in his welcome, he offered them his personally-created mélange of poteen and Provençale herbs served in exquisitely-blown Italian glasses by the side of an open fire. He lectured them on Art, the Apocalypse, and the futility of the Survival Instinct; they questioned him about his domestic arrangements, his status of confirmed bachelor ("Divorce does not EXIST!" thundered their editors on engaging them), the number of hours per week he was obliged to spend cooking and washing-up, and the brand of compost he used to grow his magnificent banks of roses. He led them from room to room pointing out his treasures – the Van Gogh drawing his dad coaxed from a restaurateur at Asnières, the scrap of authentic Inca embroidery Marie-Claude had been lucky enough to pick up (off a municipal dump near Cuzco), a pre-Cromwellian crucifix, a little-known Christmas card from Yeats to Madame Blavatsky – and, to a man, they turned their backs on the lot to hurl themselves with shrieks of delight on a hideous patchwork quilt he'd painstakingly sewn at the age of four for his mother's birthday and which he used, during his ascetic periods, as an exercise in mortification of the senses.

As the weeks went by he became accustomed to the image of himself and his work reflected from the glossy pages of the women's magazines or trudging drearily, as it were, between hedges of the newly-ordained, -conferred, -wed, and -awarded in the daily papers, or beaming sturdily from the hand-printed columns of *The Honest Craftsman* or, worst of all, shining forth like a heavenly beacon from an article on the dross and glitter of modern life in the sainted pages of *Christian Reality*. Here, they all said, was a simple unlettered countryman living out his days in the thatched white cottage where his ancestors had toiled before him, ignorant of the benefits of contemporary civilisation, of the glamorous bustle of city life, sipping his home-brewed ale in a house innocent even of central heating, cultivating a few flowers and, in his spare time, stitching away at the simple unpretentious tapestries which reflected so faithfully all the little joys and sorrows of his life. All of them cited 'Green', winner of the Bounderbury Award (though some called it 'Green Fields' and others 'Forty Shades'), a naively traditional, though still authentic, picture of his native isle.

He wrote letters to every paper, pointing out their errors of interpretation, their shocking distortion of his personality and lifestyle, then tore them up reflecting that things would fall into place when he was actually circulating among the serious artistic figures of the Capital.

Bounderbury House was all smoked glass and stainless steel without, all smoked salmon and Persian carpets within. The outside was meant to convince the slogan-loving Irish that the product on sale was fab, trendy, cool, with-it, way-out, over the top, and well worth their money; the inside to reassure tradition-conscious American buyers and EEC delegates that the Bounderbury reputation for quality combined with discreet elegance had survived inflation, union tyranny, and a multinational take-over. The name Bounderbury was synonymous not only with quality but also with generosity. There was the Bounderbury Trophy for greyhound racing, a Bounderbury crystal vase for light opera, a gold cup for show-jumping, and of course the famous Bounderbury Stakes run on Easter Monday to herald the opening of the Flat. Prizewinners were entertained lavishly in one of Paul Bounderbury's office suites in London or Dublin and, according to their presumed interests and social know-how, were thrown a couple of famous names to chew. Thus, owners and trainers invariably met the Princess Royal while faultless

Irish cavalry officers were allowed to shake hands with a junior member of the presidential family. Owing to the regrettable necessity of inviting celebrities well in advance and the assumption that all entrants for the Bounderbury Crafts Cup would be women of a certain age and uncertain intelligence, Jonathan arrived to find himself gathered to the silken bosoms of half-a-dozen assorted agony columnists, flower arrangers and romantic novelists, at the head of whom he recognised the ever-popular Diana Heartland, his first unforgettable mother-in-law and by her side her newest husband, the Hon Ralph Wetherby, retired Cabinet Minister, who smiled vaguely down at Jonathan, stroked him on the head and thundered: "Jolly good, jolly good! Well run, old chap!"

"Don't mind him, Jon darling, don't *mind* him, he thinks he's at White City. Now tell me, dear boy, when are you and that silly child Cynthia going to make up your little quarrel?"

Jonathan replied that Cynthia had not shown any sign of life for quite some time and Diana sighed: "Oh dear, she's probably found herself a sexy sheikh or a marvellous maharajah by now. I do wish the beastly gal would settle down. Too too worry-making, being a mum!"

Jonathan, reflecting that Cynthia was probably well settled down by now, or at any rate settling, wandered off to have a word with the editor of *Craft Today*. As he reached her he was intercepted by a breathlessly coy little reporter from *Hook and Loom* who trilled up at him: "And how does it feel to be here at last in Bounderbury House, surrounded by all these famous people?"

"Oo-ooh I can't believe it's weally *weal*!" Jonathan trilled back and turned to find the editor of *Craft Today* looking incredulously at him. Jonathan smiled at her and the editor addressed him with a remark of such simplistic kindness that he was instantly converted into a very small

The Prize

Black Baby accepting a sweet from a very tall White Father, then she turned away to resume her conversation about who had stabbed whom in the back at whose dinner-party.

Jonathan, slightly shaken, strolled towards the corner where the prize exhibits were hanging and introduced himself to an extraordinarily handsome young man in white bainín lounging under a gorgeous patchwork abstract.

"And I'm Oisin O'Toole," the young man murmured, his perfectly curved lips caressing his own name as his velvet eyes caressed Jonathan's body, "Aren't you going to show me your exhibit, darling?" Jonathan fled, wondering if his mother had perhaps been, after all, infallible, and made for the sanctuary of a bumptious little man in a Dunne's Stores suit who was being garrulous in a faint Ulster accent beside a piece of rather dull, though exquisitely wrought, Carrickmacross lace. Perhaps not bumptious, Jonathan thought in his chastened mood, perhaps only shy – Einstein and the photographers maybe. Hardly cosy after all, the ambience at Bounderbury House. He was about to ask the little man to nip across the road with him for a few scoops and the chat about art they were obviously not about to have with the Famous Names when silence descended on the room in the shape of a noiseless mahogany lift bearing Paul Bounderbury down from his penthouse flat to present the prizes. He did it without much fuss, being in the habit, and then the distinguished Catholic painter rose to make a speech in which she expressed her surprise and delight that all the laurels had been borne away by members of the virile sex. She commented discreetly on their physical advantages and trusted that their commitments as husbands and fathers would not prevent them from continuing to delight the public and ... ah ... herself. Jonathan collected his cup and cheque and turned to find Jenny, the coy little reporter from *Hook and Loom*, by his side. She looked so normal and healthy and undistinguished that he was quite unable to resist inviting her to dinner …

… Jenny's first, and indeed last, pregnancy was so difficult that it was only natural for her husband to take her place on the magazine. When their son was born there could be no question either of depriving him of a mother's care, so Jonathan continued working. It wouldn't be for long, Jenny said, she had great plans for his future. Of course she couldn't possibly allow him to continue with his needlework: the Bounderbury Cup had been good for a giggle but there were other, more manly, awards he could compete for. Had he thought, for example, of investing his prize-money in a couple of greyhounds and entering them for the Bounderbury Trophy? It was perhaps too late to consider opera singing (a pity, she said, with his Italian ancestry and all) but what about horses? A virile career and one she wouldn't be ashamed to discuss with the other wives over coffee. And such possibilities! The Bounderbury Stakes, Schweppes, Hennessy Gold Cup; why you could live your whole life on prize-money alone, she said, thinking of her own Auntie Bridgie, the one that married the Frenchman and kept on winning the Prix Cognac. Admittedly they gave her that for having thirty-six children but still and all it just went to show, she said, sitting up in bed with her babe at her breast, the very picture of triumphant meddling motherhood.

It was a pity to have to rob the lad of his mamma and to disturb the rosebeds again after so many years but Jonathan, about to waver, caught sight of his precious hand-reared silk chain-stitched round the neck of a nursing negligee, hardened his heart and went out for the spade. This time he was burdened with a dangerous urge to confess all, perhaps because the poor motherless bambino kept wailing away from the cradle like his conscience incarnate. It was only the thought of old Canon Kenny thundering deafly into the ears of the other penitents (HOW many times, my son?) that kept him from rushing down to the chapel. He decided instead to record it all on canvas, provide his public with the simple autobiographical tapestry it seemed to expect of him, and wait for the Gardai to knock on his door.

He was an overnight sensation. Eminent art critics wrenched copies of Roget's *Thesaurus* from one another's hands in their frantic search for original terms of hyperbolic praise. This naive descendant of the great Aubusson had turned out to be one of the immense allegorical artists of our time. A monumentally significant work of great vision and beauty, expressing as never before the agonising conflict of the human condition, Man stripping himself bare of inessentials, wrestling with and destroying one by one the hydra-headed she-devils that stood between him and his high noble destiny. (In the mood of revisionism that followed the feminist excesses of the seventies and eighties it was again acceptable to use Woman as a symbol of weakness, sloth, soulless frivolity, cowardice, and indeed any other vice that came to mind.) "But begod they're right!" Jonathan said, taking another look at his canvas and promptly accepting an invitation to lecture in the States.

For the next twenty years he was universally hailed as the master of the new century's thought. He became extremely rich and, by dint of faithfully recording on canvas all the little joys and sorrows of his life, was regarded as the initiator of a sophisticated new imagery, simplistic in appearance but possessed of such a fathomless abyss of profundity that to fully comprehend it one needed the omniscience of God combined with the black despairing wisdom of Satan himself. Before he died he saw the fulfilment of his life's work in the world-wide condemnation and indeed total rejection of painting, sculpture and other anachronistic forms of decadent art.

The end came suddenly. Invited by the French president to attend the ritual smashing of the Winged Victory he was nodding happily in his seat in time to the soothing music of pick and hammer when he felt a tap on his shoulder and turned to see the ever-popular Diana Heartland glaring at him in stony accusing horror. Unaware that this is the normal friendly expression of any woman on her fourteenth face-lift he clapped his hands to his heart, and died.

As with many great men, full understanding of Jonathan's work came only posthumously. The young couple who bought his cottage decided to modernise it, install central heating, and put down a paved yard for the kiddies to play in. They dug up the roses, took one stricken look at what lay underneath, and ran shrieking for the Guards ...

Also by Poolbeg

A Wreath upon the Dead

By

Briege Duffaud

Myth begins to unravel when Maureen Murphy, a romantic novelist who lives in a château in France, decides to base her next book on the tale of Irish folk hero, Cormac O'Flaherty. Cormac was a jockey who, in the years before the great famine of the 1840s, married his landlord's daughter, Marianne McLeod. Maureen's interest is heightened because Cormac and Marianne lived in the Claghan district of South Armagh where she herself was brought up. Her oldest friend, Kathleen O'Flaherty, is a direct descendant of the Cormac of the story.

Briege Duffaud's account of the interweaving of simple myth and complex truth in the lives of the modern O'Flahertys and McLeods makes an absolutely compelling story. Women's voices predominate in this witty, rueful and intensely readable novel which explores the national ambiguities, the facts and the fictions, of Irish life during the last sixty years. It is as eloquent about the London of the Swinging Sixties as it is about troubled Ulster.

From the voices of Maureen, Lizzie, Kathleen and Sarah we hear echoes of the sad mockery in Patrick Kavanagh's lines:

They put a wreath upon the dead
For the dead will wear the cap of any racket